Supervision

Alison Stine lives in the Appalachian foothills of Ohio. She works as a freelance writer/reporter and is an urban explorer. Her work has been published in *The Nation*, *The Paris Review*, and elsewhere. *Supervision* is her first novel. You can follow Alison on Twitter @AlisonStine

Supervision

ALISON STINE

HARPER
Voyager

HarperVoyager
An imprint of HarperCollinsPublishers Ltd
1 London Bridge Street
London SE1 9GF

www.harpervoyagerbooks.co.uk

This Paperback Original 2015

First published in Great Britain in ebook format by HarperVoyager 2015

ISBN: 978-0-00-812070-2

Set in Sabon by Born Group using Atomik ePublisher from Easypress

Printed and bound in Great Britain

*For my mom, who taught me how to read—
and for Henry, who is a Story*

CHAPTER 1

Acid Loves You

Acid walked away the day he told me that he loved me.

He said those three little words, whispered them, and then the teacher slammed her hand on my desk, making me turn around and sit up straight and pretend to pay attention. By the time I glanced back, he had slipped out of the doorway into the hall, skipping class again.

I sat in the back at school. I felt different than everyone else. I wore different clothes. My school didn't require a uniform, but I kind of wished it did. Acid wore expensive sneakers, but he'd had to scrimp for them, and I often saw him in the same shirt and jeans. Me, I was content to wear a sweatshirt, slipping the hood down over my face as far as I could, until I could hardly see.

The train the afternoon that Acid walked away was late, and when it came it was packed, only one seat in the back of the car I had chosen, near the operator's booth. It was an hour's ride home from school, forty-five minutes if I was lucky.

That was another way I was different: *I was never lucky.*

1

The subway rumbled and swayed. The car I was in emptied as more and more people got out. Hardly anyone got in as we traveled uptown. We were almost home when the train jerked and halted, and I was pushed into the sleeping man beside me. I moved away quickly, scooting over until my shoulder pressed against the side of the car. The man only snorted and went back to sleep.

The conductor's voice came over the intercom, scratchy and garbled—but I knew what he was saying; I had heard it before. "This train is being held by supervision. We will be moving shortly."

We were in between stops, and outside the window, the tunnel looked black. Inside the train, the lights flickered and went out. When they turned back on, there was something on the outside of the window.

Hand. It was a hand.

Someone was riding on the outside of the train.

I stood, my bag sliding off my lap and hitting the floor with a thud. The sleeping man grumbled. The operator came out of his booth and scanned the car.

I met his glance. "There's someone out there."

He didn't look. "Kid, sit down."

"Look!" I said.

Annoyed, he flicked his eyes in the direction I pointed, barely a glance. But the operator didn't see. "Sit down," he said. "We'll be moving soon." He opened the door to his little booth, and went back inside, muttering to himself, "Kids!"

I had heard about people riding on the outside of subway cars, trying to be funny, getting themselves killed. But when I turned to look again, to double-check, the hand was gone. I saw only the empty tunnel and the swinging work light. Why was it swinging, as if someone had knocked into it?

2

With a jerk, the train started moving again.

My stop was the last in Manhattan before the Bronx. My building was the last on the block before the highway, and our apartment was on the top floor, up five flights of stairs. No elevator. "It builds the muscles," my sister had said when she was a dancer.

But she wasn't a dancer anymore.

She was waiting for me in the hallway of the apartment when I unlocked the door, which was bad. Really bad. The Firecracker never got home before me, not since she started working her "real job," as she called it, her "grown-up job" that kept her late, every night, sometimes until nine or ten. I checked my phone. It was six.

"The Head-of-School called," the Firecracker said. "You're getting a D in English."

That hurt, but I tried not to let it. "So?" I said.

"So, they won't let you out of the ninth grade if you don't get at least a C."

I followed her into the kitchen. "What does that mean, *they won't let me out*?"

"That means, you'll lose your scholarship and be kicked out of school. You can't coast by anymore, Esmé."

"I'm not coasting," I said.

But I knew I was.

It was like I was tired all the time. It was like I was angry and upset—but if I talked to someone about it, if I stayed after school to meet a teacher or go to tutoring, I would have to think about it. I would have to bring it up. And I didn't want to bring it up. I wanted it not to be happening at all.

Miss Wrong.

I did well in school when I was a kid, well enough that they made me take tests, and the tests got me into a new

3

school, a private school. Acid and I were scholarship kids, brought in by the tests. In middle school, I had raised my hand and answered questions, and I had usually got them right. But in high school, this year, something had changed in me. I got the questions wrong sometimes, often enough that I got a new nickname.

The teachers at my new school all called us by our last names, like we were in the military or gym class. So *Wong* became *Wrong* for my classmates. *Miss Wrong.* It wasn't a stretch. It wasn't very creative.

But I still stopped raising my hand.

The Firecracker was banging pots in the kitchen. "They've given you multiple chances at that school," she said.

I dropped my bag on the floor. "No, they haven't."

"Those were their words. Not mine. Your scholarship is a big deal, and if you don't deserve it, if you don't work for it, they're going to find someone who does."

"So?" I said. I slumped against the doorframe. My sister was kneeling, her head and shoulders in a cabinet. "Are you actually going to try and cook something?" I asked.

"I'm home early," she said. "I thought I might as well."

Her frame was twisted to reach into the back of the cabinet, her arm extended, almost artfully. I thought of her dancing—and then I thought of how I was never going to see that again.

She backed out of the cabinet, holding a frying pan at a distance, as if it were something distasteful. "I can't afford that school. If you lose that scholarship, you're out."

I shrugged. "Public school."

"No. You don't understand. If you lose your scholarship, you're out of *here*. You're out of New York. I'm sending you away."

4

*

Acid never answered his phone. When it got too late to call, I fell asleep.

I had nightmares since my parents died. Not nightmares: dreams. I dreamed about a dark space. At the end of the space was a light, a bright white light growing brighter and bigger and whiter—and in the light, my mother danced.

I knew it was my mother, not my sister, although I had never actually *seen* my mother perform on stage. But the face on the dancer in my dreams matched the face I saw in pictures—like the Firecracker's only thinner, a slimmer face than mine, with the high cheekbones I would never have, and the wrinkles on the forehead I didn't have yet. It was the smile most of all that made me certain it was my mother. In photographs, she always smiled when she performed, and I knew—I remembered from seeing her on stage—my sister never did.

My sister grimaced. She grunted and frowned and stomped across the stage, a ball of energy, a lightning bolt. She danced like she was always angry. She tore through toe shoes. Her tutus ripped. Her feet bled. "The Firecracker," *The Times* called her, and the name stuck. They also wrote that she was a tribute to her mother.

My sister quit dancing, right after that.

I didn't really remember my mother, and I remembered my father only as a voice, a deep belly laugh. They died when I was a kid, in a car crash.

But I never dreamed about that.

In English, I tried to text, and the teacher saw. "Miss Wong," she said. "Your phone, please."

I slid out of my seat and dragged myself to the front. No one laughed until the third row, when a girl coughed and said it: "Miss Wrong." Then everyone laughed, an explosion that radiated through the room. The teacher glared at the class, but didn't say anything. I was getting a D, why would she?

After school, I had to double back to the classroom to pick up my phone, and I barely made the train. It was less crowded than yesterday, but slow, and the car I had picked had bad air-conditioning, the windows steaming over in the afternoon heat. Someone had cracked one open, a slit through which I could see the black tunnel. When we stopped at 168th Street, I could see something on one of the tunnel walls: graffiti. A tag. A name in bright green. I read it.

Acid.

There was more. There was a whole, terrible sentence.

Acid Loves You.

It wasn't my stop, but I pushed out of the car just as the doors were starting to close. My bag got stuck, and I yanked it free, nearly falling onto the platform. People were staring, but I didn't care.

The train began to pull away and I looked around. Everyone who had gotten off went up the stairs to street level. With a shudder, the train left too. And I could see it now, the stupid graffiti, see it clearly: *Acid Loves You.* It was painted in bright green, the color of acid, almost florescent in the dark tunnel.

The subway platform where people waited was tiled in white, but in the tunnel through which the trains traveled, the walls were black. It was here that the message had been painted. Someone had climbed down from the platform, and into the tunnel to do it.

The platform ended at the mouth of the tunnel, at a sign that read *CAUTION: DO NOT ENTER*. But a little walkway continued into the tunnel beyond the sign, an access path for subway workers. I looked down this little walkway, peering into darkness. The only light came from the work bulbs strung across the ceiling every few feet, and the signal light: a kind of traffic light for trains.

The signal light was red, which meant no train was coming.

I glanced behind me. There were only a few people waiting for the downtown train. No one was looking. I stepped over the sign, crept onto the walkway—and went into the tunnel.

I wanted to see the graffiti up close. It had to be from my friend, it *had* to be. How many people in our neighborhood were called Acid? I balanced on the narrow walkway. There was a railing, but it was low and spindly. It wouldn't hold me if I fell.

I just wouldn't fall, I told myself.

The graffiti was only a few feet inside the tunnel, painted on the wall a little above my head. Whoever had written it hadn't been much taller than me—and they were sloppy; a line of green paint trailed down the tunnel. I followed the paint splatter, crouching until I was kneeling, until the paint disappeared into the wall.

Into the wall?

I spread my palms, scanning the wall. It felt smooth. Then I felt a rough line. I worked my fingers into the crack and pulled until a door popped open. It was a small space, a crawl space, little more than a hole, and inside was darkness—and green polka dots.

Inside the door in the wall, green paint spotted the floor, so bright it glowed. I didn't think; I crawled. I pushed in, my knees dragging on cement, trying to examine the paint.

With a groan, the door to the crawl space swung shut behind me. My chest swelled and I couldn't breathe. I shot forward, knocking my forehead into a wall. Pain. Then everything was blackness.

When I woke, it took a moment for me to remember where I was. Panic returned. I was cold and stuck in the subway tunnel, in some sort of recess. I couldn't turn around so I pushed back as hard as I could, shoving my backpack against the door. It swung open and I fell out onto the tunnel walkway.

A light was moving in the tunnel, jostling up and down. I stood. I wanted to run, but I was afraid I would fall. I saw a man beneath the moving light. The light was *attached* to him, a big headlamp, and he was running, coming right at me. I would have been scared, except he looked funny with the oversized headlamp, like a kid playing dress up. He wore a pair of overalls, and they were filthy, as was his shirt. Even his face was smeared with dirt.

"Child," he said. He waved his arms. "Child, get out of here. A train is coming."

"No, it's not," I said. "The light is red."

"The light?" he said, confused.

"The signal light." I pointed behind me, then turned back to the man to show him, but he was gone. The tunnel was empty. And I felt something behind me. Arms wrapped around my waist and lifted, grabbing me, yanking me out of the tunnel.

It was another man, another subway worker who had grabbed me. He wore a bright orange and yellow safety vest, goggles, no headlamp—and there was a policewoman with him. The radio on the cop's shoulder squawked.

"We got her," the officer said into the radio.

Out on the platform, a crowd had gathered.

The subway worker was sweating. He set me down on the platform, and wiped his forehead with his hand. "Girl," he said. "You are in so much trouble."

And I was.

CHAPTER 2

Wellstone

My sister dragged the old suitcases out of the closet, and swung them onto my bed. She clicked them open, one after the other.

"What are you doing?" I asked.

"Packing," she said.

"Where are you going?"

"I'm packing for you."

"Where am *I* going?"

She looked at me. "You know."

The nightmares that night were different. No dancing. No mom. No tunnel even, despite the fact that I had just been pulled from one, despite the fact that the police had taken me to a corner of the station, and asked me: *What was I doing? How could I have been so dumb? Didn't I know I could have been killed? Didn't I know people died that way? Just a few months ago, in this very tunnel.*

I knew, I knew, I told them. I said I was sorry.

The first few times I told the story, I told about the man with the headlamp and the dirty clothes. But no one knew who the

10

man was. So I stopped telling that part. When my sister showed up, the police let me go. No fine. This time. And no court appearance because the Firecracker was taking me out of state.

She promised.

The nightmares that night felt real. I dreamed I was in my bed in my room in the apartment—but something was wrong with my hand. It hurt. It tingled, the blood pricking my palm as if my hand had fallen asleep.

But then in the dream, when I turned over to look at it on the sheet, my hand wasn't there. It just wasn't there. My hand was gone. It hurt, but it was a phantom pain. In my dream, my body was missing.

I woke up with aches, my limbs stiff from sleeping wrong— and I woke up late. The Firecracker threw my suitcases down the stairs. I pulled on an oversized sweatshirt and jeans without looking in the mirror, half-asleep.

It was May, still cold in the morning. We didn't talk in the cab. We didn't hug at the station. I kept my hands stuffed in my pockets and my hood pulled down.

But then the Firecracker said, "It will be better this time."

I sniffed. "What do you mean?"

"Grandma. She'll be good for you. It'll be good for you to be in the country right now, away from ..." she gestured around at the station: the early morning commuters rushing by, the platform littered with trash, the garbage cans covered with graffiti like scabs. "All this."

"I thought you loved all this."

"Sometimes I do," my sister said. "But it's time for you to go."

And then she gripped my shoulders and pulled me toward her in a hug. She smelled of fancy perfume and leather and the smell that never quite went away from her; it seemed

11

attached to her hair, the smell of rosin for the toe shoes, though it had been ages since she had worn them.

"I'll visit you soon," the Firecracker said. I was about to say something in response, but then she pulled out of the hug and squeezed my shoulder. "Esmé, eat something. You feel like you're wasting away to nothing."

Once on the train, I closed my eyes and didn't look back.

My sister had bought me a ticket on the Keystone to Pennsylvania—a daylong trip from Penn Station. I slept mostly. We passed into New Jersey, following the water, steely and gray. I didn't talk to anyone, or move when the conductor came through, calling for lunch reservations. I wasn't hungry. When the train stopped after Elizabethtown, at the most desolate, busted place I could imagine, I stood. This was the stop. I knew it. After all, I had been here before.

When our parents died, the Firecracker was fifteen—my age now—too young to take care of me herself. I tried to imagine my sister like me, in school, wearing toe shoes around her neck, her long hair in a ponytail. I couldn't picture it, not really. I was five then, and we moved in with our grandmother, our mother's mother, for three years until my sister was legal, could drop out of school and get a job, get a place for us back in the city where we belonged, she said.

I knew the blandness, the brokenness of this place, I had been here and escaped from it once already. Wellstone.

The conductor called the name of the town, but I was the only one who got out. The train huffed away, and I was left. Outside on the platform, under an overhang, I sat on a bench to wait.

Wellstone was a punishment, like my grandmother was a punishment. My sister had used both of them as idle threats for years. If I didn't do better in school, if I didn't come home on time, if I didn't stop talking back, she would send me here, to Wellstone, where there were no malls or coffee shops or stores that stayed open past five o'clock or kids my own age or anything to do.

There were also rumors about this town, stories which I could still remember bits of: something about a man in the woods; bones in the weeds; places where kids were afraid to play. This was not a good place, I knew that much.

My grandmother didn't have internet. She didn't have a computer. She didn't have cable. She lived in an old, rambling mansion that was falling down. It wasn't *safe*, I remembered. Once, my foot had fallen through a stair. Rain had fallen through the ceiling. The Firecracker had cried a lot.

But in New York, after they had pulled me from the tunnel, my sister had made plans, secretly and instantly. There were three weeks left of school, and she had arranged for me to be transferred. The school in Wellstone had emailed a schedule. They were expecting me.

Grandma was the only family we had left, the last resort for me.

I didn't even know if I would know her face. She was quiet and terrifying, I remembered that much. She kept cats with no tails who roamed freely in and out of the house. There was a barn I wasn't allowed to go into. There was a big black bag she carried that I wasn't allowed to touch.

My grandmother had worked the night shift, as a nurse or something. She had cooked strange things, nearly inedible things, bubbling stews and simmering broths, which she left hissing on the stove all day. The house smelled of herbs and dried flowers and dust and spice and boiling chickens. She kept the bones. The cats played with them.

13

On the train platform, I shivered. I checked for reception on my phone. I waited. And I waited. I had started to fall asleep when I heard a car. I sat up and reached for my suitcases.

My grandmother came around the corner of the station. I hadn't seen her for seven years. She was smaller than I remembered, and she wore glasses, the kind with a beaded chain. She walked heavily and slowly, as though it hurt her. She stepped up to the platform and looked across.

I didn't run to her. I didn't shout. I wasn't going to hug her. I decided to stay very still. I decided to look like it didn't matter; I didn't care.

She turned, and without a word to me, began to walk back to her car.

"Grandma?" I said, but my voice felt thick. I wasn't sure she had heard me. By the time I had gathered up my bags, the car was starting. "Grandma, no!" I left the suitcases and ran into the parking lot.

Her car, a station wagon, was just disappearing up the road.

I dialed my phone. "Grandma left me," I said when my sister picked up.

"Why are you calling me at work?"

"She *left* me."

"Where?" my sister said.

"At the train station."

"Well, was your train late?"

"No."

"I'm sure it's a mistake," the Firecracker said. "A misunderstanding."

I remembered her raging about our grandmother, about her strangeness, her habits. *Eccentric* was the word the Firecracker used, which, as a child, I had thought was *electric*; I kept waiting for our grandmother to light up like a Christmas tree.

"You know where she lives," my sister said.

"No, I don't."

"Well, you have the address. And you remember the house."

"Yes," I said.

I couldn't forget the house.

I hung up the phone, hoisted my suitcases, and started up the hill to the road. Soon a truck passed me, a group of bare-chested boys hanging out in the bed. Wellstone boys. I thought about hitchhiking, though the Firecracker would kill me if she found out, but the truck didn't slow.

I began to remember the way. Past the gas station and fairgrounds. There was the hill. There was the road, the driveway cracked and steep. I tightened my grip on the suitcases and started up. The driveway veered, and there was the house: glowering from on top of the hill. The house was three stories, mostly brick, and over a hundred years old. It had belonged to someone important. It had been passed down. It had a name—but I couldn't remember what it was.

I passed my grandmother's station wagon parked in front of the collapsing barn. When the driveway ended, I dragged my suitcases through the grass, tearing through the weeds to get around the house. The grass hadn't been mowed in a long time, and there were tree limbs down all over the yard. Wide steps led to a front porch and double doors, thrown wide open to the afternoon. When I walked up the steps, four blurs shot out of the doors and down, yowling.

Cats. My grandmother fed a whole herd of them, all tailless. *Manx*, I remembered they were called.

"Scat!" I told them. I dropped my suitcases on the porch and knocked at the open door. "Grandma?" I called.

No one answered.

I went inside.

I hadn't remembered how high the ceilings of the house were, how the wooden floors echoed. I peeked in the doorway of the first room to my left: empty, except for bookshelves and a piano. The room on the right, the dining room, had a heavy oak table in the center, drapes drawn shut over the windows, and a fireplace, the marble mantle cluttered with candles. There were candles on the floor in the hallway too, all dusty and blackened, burned down to nubs.

A ballroom stood on the third floor, I remembered now—I had roller skated there. A big staircase led up to it, but I kept walking down the hall. I came to a smaller set of stairs, the servant steps. To my right was the kitchen. To my left was the sitting room where my grandmother waited for me, watching television with the sound off.

"Grandma?" I whispered.

Blue light flickered over her face. It was her. She was the same, only shrunken, only not speaking to me for some reason.

"I'm here," I said.

She didn't say anything.

"Esmé? Jennifer's daughter?"

It hurt to say my mother's name. Not *hurt* exactly. It felt forbidden, like a spell. It felt like I shouldn't speak her name aloud. I wished I hadn't. I felt dizzy, like I might be sick.

Her face unfroze at the sound of my and my mother's names. She looked around, concentrating, as if she was listening hard. I thought she was going to speak. But she only reached over to the end table, picked a phone, saw that nobody had called or was calling, and turned the phone facedown again. She never met my eyes.

I turned away. "I'll just go get my bags," I said.

I lugged them up the main stairs because I didn't want to have to face her again. Was she mad at me already? What had my sister said to her about me?

On the second floor, there were four closed doors, and two open ones. The front room held a white canopied bed. There were magazines and old, moldy books on the night table, and house slippers underneath it—my grandmother's room.

That left the smaller room for me. I was relieved to see the bed had sheets on it, a pink quilt folded at the foot, towels draped over a chair. I opened the two doors in the room to find a closet, and a bathroom with a tub ringed in rust.

Had this been my room? I set my suitcases down, opened the drapes at the window, and looked out. The room faced the backyard. Beyond the old barn, there was a pond, round and still. I hadn't remembered that, either.

Exhausted, too worn out to be hungry, I climbed into bed and pulled the quilt around me. I didn't bother getting undressed, or calling the Firecracker to tell her I was here. Not *home*. I was not home. I would never say that word again.

I was too nervous to sleep beyond the first beam of sun breaking through the drapes. Despite weak water pressure, the shower worked. I combed out my long hair, pulled on a new shirt and jeans. The door to my grandmother's bedroom was closed, and downstairs, there was no sign of her. I remembered her working nights, remembered the Firecracker making dinner, and grumbling about it. I found a bowl and cereal in the cabinet, milk in the fridge. I ate standing up over the sink, then washed and dried my dishes, putting them away where I had found them.

I wouldn't bother my grandmother. I wouldn't be a burden; she wouldn't notice me at all.

The school bus stop was at the bottom of the driveway, my sister had told me, and a handful of kids already stood out there by the road. One of the boys looked up as I approached. One of the girls was studying a book, and another boy tried to knock it out of her hands.

She snatched it away. "I've got a test."

"New girl today," the boy said.

I adjusted my bag. I just wanted to get this over with. "I'm Esmé," I said.

"Weird name," he said.

"Weird *family*," a second girl said.

"Do you think she's a witch like her grandma?" the boy asked.

I held my bag tighter. "My grandma's not a witch," I said.

"All I know is," the girl with the book said, "this girl got kicked out of her old school. She's like, a juvenile delinquent or something. A total freak."

"I am not," I said.

But the boy just lunged for the girl's book again. They wrestled, the girl smacking the boy on the shoulder, the other girl ignoring them, examining the split ends of her hair. I stood at the back of the bus line, hating this place, and hating my grandmother and my sister for bringing me here.

When the bus came, I sat in the first empty seat, and no one sat with me or talked to me. When we stopped and the bus emptied, I had to fight to get out into the aisle; kids kept pushing past me, and the driver almost closed the door.

I wasn't sure if I was supposed to check in, but I waited around the office for what seemed like forever, until after the first warning bell had sounded and the office cleared. Then I followed the late kids out into the hall. No one asked if they could help me or what I was doing. I didn't bother finding my locker. I pulled the print-out of my schedule from my pocket, and was searching for room numbers when the tardy bell rang.

Someone sprinted around a corner and plowed into me.

I was knocked to my knees. My bag shot off my back and onto the floor, the zipper splitting open. The boy who had knocked me down pushed himself up with a squeal of his sneakers and took off. "Hey," I said. "I'm fine. Thanks."

He dashed around the next corner and was gone.

"Jerk," I said.

In the empty hallway, I stood and gathered my stuff. I collected the loose papers that had fallen from the folder that was supposed to travel with me to the office: my permanent record from New York. Words leapt out at me from the file: *distracted … disrespectful … loner … antisocial … underachiever … daydreamer … lives in a fantasy world …*

The words began to blur. No, I would not cry. Not on the first day of school. I shoved the pages back into the folder. Somehow, I found my classroom. A science lab. Students perched at tables, looking bored. There was one empty stool so I took it.

"All right," the teacher said. She looked up. She was going to make some sort of announcement, introduce me, something embarrassing.

I tensed, waiting for it.

The door shot open and a boy came in, looking flustered. He headed straight for me.

He ran up to me. Then he *sat* on me—or tried to, sat right on my stool, on my lap. I pushed him as hard as I could,

19

and he tumbled off the stool onto the ground. He looked up, his face blanching.

The class laughed, everyone at once. The teacher rolled her eyes and told them to be nice, told the boy to be more careful. He stood and reached for my stool again, and I backed up, scooting the stool with me.

"Sit in the back, Ron," the teacher said. "I don't think that chair likes you."

"The chair?" I said. "Hello? I have a name."

But Ron moved away, and no one asked me what my name was. The teacher didn't do an announcement, or give me a book. She didn't even take roll. She started the class like nothing was different. "So," she said. "Today we're going to talk about something that actually matters to us, matters to our history here in Wellstone."

"History matters?" some boy said.

"The locomotive," the teacher said. "You might be surprised to learn the steam locomotive has something in common with an aircraft carrier. Anyone know what?"

I looked around. No one knew my name here yet. No one knew my nickname—*Miss Wrong*—or had given it to me, thinking they were being smart, thinking they were being new. Slowly I raised my hand.

"The steam locomotive and an aircraft carrier. What do they have in common?"

I pumped my hand. I waved it.

"Anyone?" the teacher said.

"Excuse me?" I said. "They both convert heat into motion."

The teacher sighed. "They both convert heat into motion."

I lowered my hand.

"Take out your books," the teacher said. "I know we've all got senioritis here, but there are three weeks left of school and we're going to make them count. Read chapter twelve to yourselves, please, then we'll do the questions together."

Everyone fumbled with their books. Everyone but me.

I waited for the teacher to notice. I waited for her to give me a book, to ask my name, to *see* me. But she never did.

CHAPTER 3

Six Feet

I raised my hand once in my next class, English, and in the next, Geometry. And then I gave up. I sat out on the bleachers during gym, and no one said anything. At lunch, I sat alone at a table near the back until it was swarmed with cheerleaders in pleated skirts and ponytails, chattering around me.

At home, I was mocked. I was made fun of. But here, I was ignored. I was invisible.

This was worse.

No one spoke to me the whole day until, on the bus ride home, a girl sat down in the seat in front of me. I was watching the window, the gray sameness of the landscape, when her head popped up above the seat. "You must be completely new," she said.

I glanced up. Was she actually speaking to me? The girl had long blond hair in waves, and severe features. Her eyebrows were black, a shocking contrast to her hair. She was not smiling.

I cleared my throat. "I got here yesterday."

"I figured. Completely green. So, why are you here?"

"What do you mean?"

"What happened to get you sent here? What did you do?"

I studied the girl. "What did *you* do?"

She smiled. "My mother was otherwise occupied. She was working, couldn't be bothered. And then, well, I went somewhere I wasn't supposed to go, didn't I."

I smiled. "Me too. Something like that, anyway. I'm Esmé Wong."

"Strange name," the girl said.

"What's yours?"

"Clara Blue."

That name wasn't exactly normal, I thought.

All around us on the bus, kids laughed and messed around, trying to shove each other off the seats. But Clara Blue studied me, serious and calm. The bus plowed over a bump in the road, and she barely moved. "Well, you're obvious, Esmé Wong," she said. "You need to work on that. I'll help you, don't worry." Then she turned back around.

I couldn't stop smiling. I had made a friend, one friend. My stop was next and when I passed Clara's seat, I paused to say goodbye to the girl, but her seat was empty. The bus driver was about to close the doors so I hurried down the aisle and exited. With a jerk, the bus pulled away. Something made me turn to look at it.

Clara's face peered at me from the window, round as the moon.

It got hot in the afternoon. By the time I reached the top of the hill, my T-shirt clung to me and I had taken off my hoodie. Grandma's station wagon was gone, and the house was blissfully empty. I went into the kitchen to look for something to eat, chasing away the cats who perched on the

23

counter, hissing at me. I checked my phone. A message from the Firecracker. I called her back.

"Where are you?" she asked.

"Wellstone," I said. "Grandma's creepy old house."

"Well, she called me this morning. At work. She said you never showed."

"I'm here," I said. "I went to that stupid school today. I rode the stupid bus. Grandma's mad at me for something. Or maybe she needs her bifocals changed."

"Esmé," my sister said. "What's going on? Are you at Grandma's or aren't you?"

"I'm here. And it sucks. So when are you going to end this, and bring me home?"

"No," she said. "You're staying. You two have to work it out. You and Grandma have to talk. It's better for you to be there."

I hung up the phone, and drank a glass of water from the tap. It tasted funny, like copper. I looked around. The kitchen was dark and cluttered. A fireplace in the corner. On each of the ceiling beams hung a cluster of drying flowers or herbs. At the back of the kitchen was a door that led to nowhere, three feet of empty space outside where steps should have been, but were never built.

The house was full of little things like that, half-finished rooms, stairs that led up into ceilings. That door in the kitchen was always locked, I remembered, to keep someone from falling. I glanced out the window over the sink, where the pond sparkled in the sun.

In one of my suitcases, I found a swimsuit. Under the porch, I found a blue plastic raft. Barefoot, I walked down to the pond, and set the raft in the water. It floated. I hesitated for only a moment, then I got on.

I drifted toward the center of the pond, which was small, probably used to water cows. I thought I remembered cows, though there was no sign of them now. On the other side of the pond was a fenced-in pasture, overgrown with weeds, then hill after hill of trees. The ones closest to the pond were birches, white bark reflecting the sun. Cattails grew at the pond's edge, gummed in mud.

I closed my eyes. The sun felt good on my face. I wished I had thought to bring a book. I floated for a while, listening to the birds. I almost fell asleep. Then I heard a voice.

"You shouldn't be in there."

I opened my eyes and sat up.

A boy stood on the opposite bank of the pond by the cattails. He was tall. He had black hair, and the bluest eyes I had ever seen, blue as pool water, blue as broken glass. He was staring at me. "Someone drowned in there," he said.

"What? Here?" I tried to pull my suit down. I felt cold and exposed.

"That pond. It's unlucky."

"I can swim."

"I'm sure you can. Only I'm not sure it'll matter."

"Oh," I said. I wished I had a towel, something with which to cover myself. I slid off the raft, intending to stand in the water.

But the water was deeper than I expected, and I didn't touch bottom. I slipped, muddy water splashing up to my neck, into my mouth. I reached for the raft, but the raft danced away.

I felt arms beneath me, hands grasping my shoulders. The boy carried me to the bank by the birches. He tried to lay me on the ground, but I scrambled up.

"I can stand," I said. "I'm fine."

25

The boy wore long shorts, cut ragged at the knees, a button-down shirt, and no shoes. All his clothes were soaking now.

"Thanks," I said. "I guess the water was deeper than I thought."

"Told you," he said. "Unlucky." He put his hands in his pockets and turned.

He was actually going to leave. Just carry me out of a cow pond and leave.

I called to the boy. "Wait. Who drowned here?"

"A man. A man at a party. A long time ago."

"How do you know?"

"I'm your neighbor, Tom Griffin. And you're Esmé, I know." He ducked under the fence, cutting through the pasture. "Clara told me all about you. She tells me everything." He grinned at me, then was gone behind a birch.

I stared after him, waiting for him to reappear on the other side of the tree, but he didn't. I ran through the moment in my head. He was my neighbor, had maybe saved me from drowning, had the bluest eyes I thought I had ever seen.

And he had a girlfriend.

I saw Tom the next day in school.

Or rather: he saw me, which was significant because *no one* noticed me, not all day. My grandmother was asleep when I left. The bus doors nearly closed on my back. My teachers ignored me, and nobody talked to me—at least nobody tried to sit on me again either—until lunchtime. As I scanned the crowded room, holding my sack lunch, an apple rolled across the cafeteria to rest against my foot.

I bent and picked it up. It was a green apple, sour, the kind I liked best. I looked up. Tom stood on the other side of the cafeteria by the windows. I paused for a moment, then took my lunch and went over to him.

"Come sit at our table," he said.

"I didn't know you went to this school. *Our* table?"

He pushed open the door that led into the courtyard, motioning for me to go ahead.

"Outside?" I asked. "I didn't think we were allowed to eat outside."

"Oh, trust me," a female voice said. "No one will notice."

It was Clara. My heart began to beat faster.

"People just rush through this courtyard on their way to class," Tom said. "But I think it's nice out here. Quiet. We can talk." He pointed to the bench where Clara sat, smoothing the skirt of her dress. It looked expensive and delicate, the color of ice. Tom wore almost the same clothes as yesterday.

With a pang, I thought of Acid. My old school, my old life.

Then I looked closer at Tom. I wondered how he could get away with wearing shorts at school, which was not allowed. I wondered how long the three of us could sit out here in the courtyard, which was also not allowed; we were clearly visible through the windows of the cafeteria.

"Aren't you worried about getting in trouble?" I asked.

"No," Tom said.

"We got over that a long time ago," Clara said. "I guess you haven't yet."

"Why didn't I see you here yesterday?" I asked Tom.

But Clara was the one who answered. "He comes to school when he feels like it."

I had sat on the bench beside her, noting that Tom took the place on her other side. They were familiar with each other, casual and comfortable. He bumped Clara's shoulder. She made a face at him. They wore the same kind of shoes, black leather lace-ups that looked expensive, though the leather was dusty and cracked.

I took a bite of my sandwich. "How long have you guys been together?"

"Together?" Tom said.

"A long time," Clara said.

Tom looked at her, then at me. He looked like he was trying not to laugh. "We're *siblings*."

Then Clara did laugh.

I swallowed. I felt heat in my face. "But you have different last names?"

"We're adopted," Clara said.

"We've known each other since we were kids," Tom said. "We grew up together. That's all."

"Oh. Okay." I held my sandwich out. "Do either of you want half?"

Tom looked like he was going to laugh again. "No, thanks."

Clara exchanged a glance with him. "She's so sweet. Look at her trying."

I felt stupid for a reason I didn't understand. I balled up the wax paper from the sandwich, crumpled my napkins. Tom and Clara hadn't eaten anything at all. "How do you stand it here?" I asked them. "Everyone ignores me. I feel like I'm being shunned."

"You get used to it," Clara said. "It becomes easier."

"I feel like I'm going crazy. I don't know what I did."

Tom tilted his head strangely. "What *did* you do?"

"What do you mean?"

"What happened to you, to end up here?"

I stood. Clara had asked me the same question on the bus. "What is this place?" I asked. "You have to commit a crime to be sent here? No, I didn't do anything wrong. I didn't do anything. There's nothing wrong with me." Conscious that Tom and Clara were watching, I dumped my lunch in a trashcan, and went back into the cafeteria, where I sat alone in silence until the bell rang.

Tom and Clara weren't on the afternoon bus.

I got a snack in the empty house, glancing through the window at the backyard. Tom had said we were neighbors, but the closest house was far down the road, past the fair-grounds. When I had passed it on my walk from the train station, an old woman had been out front, pulling weeds. Did she have two adopted teenagers?

I washed my dishes and put them away. I was heading up the stairs to take a nap, or start on the homework no one would ever collect from me, when I heard a crash.

It was an old house. It made sounds, creaking and groaning, settling, especially at night. It was also overrun with cats, and given my grandmother's tendency to leave the doors wide open, possibly other strays as well.

There was another crash, followed by a muffled curse.

"Hello?" I said.

At the top of the stairs a door had been flung open: the door to the linen closet, its shelves stuffed with junk. Someone was at the bottom of the closet, searching on hands and knees. "Nuts!" the figure said.

"Excuse me?" I said.

The figure turned. It was a girl, barely older than me. Seeing me, she jumped and clutched at her chest. She wore a drab brown dress and a dingy apron. On her head she had fastened a little white hat. "You gave me a fright," she said. "Miss, don't do that."

"I'm sorry. Who are you again?"

She sat back on her heels. "I'm Martha."

"Okay," I said. "Martha. What are you doing in the closet?"

"Well, I thought it was time to change your bedclothes."

"Change the bedclothes?" I stared at the girl, her dress and apron, that hat. "Grandma has a *maid*? Since when?"

"A long time," the girl—the maid—said.

"Do you live here?"

Martha nodded.

That was news to me. I definitely hadn't remembered a maid. "Why haven't I seen you before?"

"It's a big house," Martha said. "And your grandmother is awfully particular about what I do and when I do it."

"She sure has a lot of stuff to clean," I said, staring past Martha into the closet, which was crammed with sheets, bolts of fabric, glassware, and candles. So many candles. On the bottom shelf, there appeared to be a trumpet. A trumpet? I thought of how dusty the house was; how cobwebs were practically knitted in the corners, thick and gray; how the sides of my bathtub bled with rust.

Martha the maid didn't seem particularly good at her job.

"I don't mind," Martha said.

I studied her. "Um, are you old enough to be a maid?"

"Old enough." Martha stood, groaning as she rose, as if to prove it. "Back to work for me. You run along now. I bet your friends are outside waiting."

"My friends?" I said. "Clara? Tom?"

But the front yard was empty. A cat, dozing on a downed limb, stared at me with one open yellow eye. I was about to go down to the pond—maybe Martha meant the backyard—when I saw the man in the driveway. He stood by the road, looking up toward the house, but when he noticed me, he turned quickly away.

30

I wandered down the driveway. "Can I help you?" I asked.

The man wore all black. His hair was black too, a shaggy mess, and his skin looked waxen—as washed-out as Tom and Clara had looked, I realized. People didn't seem to get much sun in Wellstone.

"Are you looking for my grandmother?" I asked.

The man looked miserable, purple shadows under his eyes, which were swollen into slits and bloodshot. "I believe I may have left something at your house," he mumbled.

"Okay, I'll go ask my grandma." I didn't want to tell him she wasn't home.

"I believe I may have lost something. In your pond."

"Seriously?"

"Lily pads, coy. Nice gazebo."

"There's no gazebo."

"There was to be a fountain in the middle—but we never got that far."

"I think you've got the wrong pond," I said. I started to back up the hill. I wondered if the maid was watching from the windows, if she could hear me if I screamed.

The man peered at the house. But there was a faraway look in his eyes. "I remember that pond. I designed it."

"No one designed it. It's just a pond."

"I believe I may have lost something in that pond."

"Look," I said. "I'm going to call my grandma—"

"I believe I may have drowned in that pond."

I turned and ran up the driveway.

Two figures were coming down toward me from the direction of the house: Tom and Clara. "Hey," I said, waving my arms. "We need to call the cops. There's a guy down there. A crazy guy."

"Where?" Tom said.

31

I turned to show him.

But the man was gone. I hadn't seen a car, hadn't heard an engine. There was no one in the road. A breeze rustled through the trees, knocking branches together, drifting my hair in front of my face. I realized I was shaking.

"Are you all right?" Tom asked.

"She's green," Clara said. "Completely green. I told you, Tom. She needs us."

"There was a man," I said. "I swear it."

"I believe you," Tom said. "What did he look like?"

"Strange. Black hair. Black clothes."

They exchanged a glance.

"What?" I said.

"We know him," Tom said. "He's a character. Harmless, though."

"Completely rolled," Clara said.

"Harmless, Esmé," Tom repeated.

And I *felt* something when he said my name. It was a sudden lift, like a weight had been taken from me, like I had felt in the tunnel when the subway worker had pulled me away, before I knew what was happening, before I knew the fallout; I had thought I was flying.

Tom held out his hand. "Come on. We want to tell you something."

Tom held my hand most of the way. His touch felt light and tenuous, like I was trying to hold onto a leaf. We walked behind the house, by the pond. I tried not to look at it as we passed. It was only an ugly old pond. Stories were just stories.

Clara led us around the back of the barn, then stopped. "We're here."

"What's here?" I asked.

Tom dropped my hand. "A home base, of sorts. At least for Clara."

We stood in the grass by the barn before an oak tree with big exposed roots. At the base of the trunk rested a pile of old bricks with a hole at the middle, like a pizza oven. Protruding from the top of the brick pile was a chimney.

"It's a kiln," Tom said. "Not used anymore, if it ever was. It's just the secret entrance to a tunnel."

"A what?" I said.

"That's what we want to show you. It's one of Clara's favorite places. It's perfectly safe," he said when I looked at him. "Come on. Clara will go first."

Clara hiked her skirt with one hand, and bent under the archway of bricks, into the mouth of the kiln. She gave a trilling whistle, like a bird. Then she was gone.

"Whoa," I said.

"It's just a tunnel, Ez."

"I don't do so great with tunnels."

"It's just a way in. And there are steps in there, a ladder. You don't even have to jump. Come on. I'll help you."

What had he called me?

Ez.

No one had ever called me that before.

Tom took my hand, and led me into the kiln. At first, all I saw was blackness, then I could make out some kind of passageway a few feet below. Something protruded from the wall: a ladder made of bricks. I clutched Tom's hand, and with my other, reached blindly. My fingers found a brick. I let go of Tom and called, "I've got it."

"Finally," Clara muttered below me.

I climbed down the ladder, Tom following close behind. When I leapt from the last step, I landed on packed earth, and moved over for Tom, who jumped down beside me. "How far down are we?" I asked.

"Six feet," Tom said.

I thought of the barn, six feet above us, the fields, the pond.

"This way," Tom said.

He was holding my hand again. We moved forward, crouching for a few dim steps, then my eyes adjusted, the tunnel opened, and I could stand upright. The passageway extended for as long as I could see, wide enough for Tom, Clara, and me to stand abreast.

"What is this place?" I asked. My voice was a whisper, but it bounced off the walls.

"What it was," Tom said, "was part of the Underground Railroad."

"Really? I thought that was just an expression. Not actual tunnels."

"There were some tunnels."

"Is it safe? How long does it go on?"

"All the way to your grandmother's house."

"My grandmother's house was a stop on the Underground Railroad?"

It made sense. The house was old enough.

And big and strange enough.

I touched the smooth brick walls of the tunnel with my hand. The air felt cold and thin. The subway tunnel came back to me then: the darkness, the door, the pain in my forehead when I had struck the wall. I pressed on my temples. "Wait," I said. "You said this is *home*? A home base? You live here?" I thought of Tom's clothes, how raggedy they were, how he had worn the same outfit. "Are you runaways?"

My eyes had adjusted fully now. I could see the dirt floors of the tunnel, packed and swept. Clean, as clean as floors of dirt

34

could be. But bare. There were no sleeping bags, no blankets, no signs of food, no signs of life. How were they living here?

"Why?" I said. "Why did you run away? Where are your parents?"

"Don't know anymore," Tom said.

"Do you have enough to eat? How long have you been down here?"

"It's fine, Ez," Tom said, more softly. "We're fine."

"Is it safe? Is someone looking for you?"

"Yes," Clara said. She was right up next to me. She smelled of talcum powder and dirt, and there were circles under her eyes, wide and purple as the circles under the eyes of the man in the driveway. "Someone is looking. And he finds us just about every night."

"Stop it, Clara," Tom said. "You're scaring her."

I hugged my arms to my chest. I was freezing.

"Are you all right?"

"Just cold," I said.

"No, you're not," Clara said.

"Excuse me?"

"Clara," Tom said.

But she answered, "We're not helping her. She has to know." Clara turned to me. "You're not cold. You're not hungry. You're not thirsty. You're just tired." She stood right in my face, her eyes hard. "Stop pretending to be those other things. You can't be those other things anymore, not ever again. Just tired. All you'll ever be is tired. And you'll never get to sleep. Never."

I shook my head. The air felt too thin. The brick ceiling too close. I needed to get away from Clara, out of the tunnel. "I don't know what you mean," I said. I backed up until my shoulder hit a wall. The cold, damp brick was like an electric shock against my skin. I gasped.

35

"Oh for heaven's sake," Clara said.

"It's all right," Tom said. "Forgive us, Ez. We've never done this before."

"Done what?" I said.

"Told someone."

"Told someone *what*?"

Why weren't they hungry? Why were they running? Why were they tired all the time?

"We're dead," Tom said. "And so are you."

CHAPTER 4

I'm Alive

I flew out of the tunnel. I couldn't get out fast enough. I barely remember climbing the ladder, but somehow my fingers found the brick holds. Then I was coughing in the sunlight, gasping for air. Tom followed me out.

"You're sick," I said to him. "Sick."

He stood over me. "It's true, what I said."

"That's not funny. You're a jerk like everyone else in this town."

He touched my shoulder. I started to shrug him off, then I grabbed his arm by the wrist. "See?" I said. "You're real. Real as me." I shook his arm. It went limp in my hand. "I can touch you. I can feel you. You're solid, just like me."

"Because we're both *dead*. You can touch me because *you're* dead too."

Clara had come out of the kiln and stood watching by the tree.

"Help me out," Tom said to her.

"Oh, I don't think so. I already tried. Besides, you've had more experience."

"Experience?" I said.

"He died before me."

I flung Tom's arm away. I felt shaky. I needed to talk to someone normal, the Firecracker, the maid. I started toward the house, but Tom followed me, motioning to Clara to do the same.

"Leave me alone!" I said to them. "What's wrong with you? What is this—gang up on the new girl? I haven't been hazed enough? Someone trying to sit on me in school wasn't enough?"

Tom halted. "Someone tried to sit on you?"

I stopped too.

Tom's voice was patient, low. "No one talked to you in school, did they, Ez? The teachers didn't notice you. Your grandmother didn't even say hello to you."

"I—I," I stumbled. My mind was spinning. "Martha talked to me! My grandmother's maid."

"Martha?" Clara stood at my elbow. "She's been dead a century."

I tried to remember what the maid had said. She knew my grandmother. She seemed to know me. And the house was always dusty, the stairs un-swept, the bathroom moldy. Martha said she had worked in the house … forever.

I thought back over the last two days: the school bus doors nearly closing on me every time I rode, the boy trying to sit on me, the other boy running me down in the hall. I remembered Clara, appearing out of nowhere on the bus, and Tom materializing on the bank of the pond then disappearing behind a birch.

I felt clammy and cold. I felt for my arms. I could feel them. I kicked my legs. I felt solid to me. I remembered the nightmare the night before I had left New York, when I had thought my hand was gone—but that was just a dream. I had those kinds of dreams a lot, along with the dreams of my mother, dreams where people were shouting at me, shaking me, dreams where I woke up feeling choked.

"The Firecracker!" I said.

Tom and Clara stared at me.

"My sister. Her nickname is the Firecracker. I talked to her just yesterday. I talk to her every day. She wouldn't be able to talk to me if I were dead." I had already pulled out my phone and was dialing. *Please pick up, please pick up, please, please,* I begged her in my head. "Oh thank you!" I said when she answered.

"What?" she said. "What's wrong? Did something happen?"

I put the phone on speaker and held it out to Tom and Clara.

"Esmé?" the Firecracker said, her voice crackling. "Esmé, are you there?"

"See?" I said.

Tom and Clara just looked at me. Clara seemed unimpressed. But Tom looked frightened. His eyes were on me, not on the phone, as the Firecracker's voice blared: "What's going on? Is everything okay over there?"

"Everything's fine. You're speaking to me, I'm fine, and everything is fine."

"Okay," the Firecracker said. "That's not suspicious."

"I just met some people, and they didn't believe some things about me."

"I'm really glad you're making friends. Listen, I've got to get back to work, okay?"

"Sure," I said. "Love you too." I snapped the phone shut. "See?"

But Tom shook his head. "No. Something is wrong. You wouldn't be able to interact with us. You wouldn't be able to touch us unless you were like us. Unless you were dead too. That's how we found Martha. And Mr. Black."

"Who's Mr. Black?" I asked.

There was the sound of a car then, creeping up the driveway. We all turned to see my grandmother's station wagon pull up in front of the barn.

"I've an idea," Clara said.

"No," Tom said. "She's not ready."

"How else is she going to *get* ready? How will she ever believe us otherwise?"

"What are you going to do?" I asked.

My grandmother got out of the station wagon, balancing a grocery bag on her hip. She set another bag on the ground as she closed the car door.

I whispered, "Grandma?"

She picked up the other bag, pausing for a moment, as if she had noticed or just remembered something. Her face took on the look it had taken in the sitting room. Concentration, mixed with a strange sort of blankness. She stared into the woods in the distance. Then she blinked and shook her head, as if shaking off a memory, coming out of a trace.

"Grandma," I said.

Without hearing me, she headed for the house. But Clara blocked her path. Reaching out, the girl plucked something from my grandmother's grocery bag: a carton of eggs.

"What are you doing?" I asked.

"She can't see me. She can't see you. But she can see this." Clara opened the carton and pulled out an egg. She tossed it to Tom, who caught it.

"Clara, stop." He set the egg gently on the ground.

"You're no fun." Clara took another egg from the carton.

My grandmother watched the eggs, transfixed.

"Stop it," I said.

"Fine," Clara said, and she dashed the egg against the house. The egg broke against the wall with a sickening smack, yellow sliding down the side. My grandmother flinched. She tightened her hold on the grocery bag. But Clara wasn't done. She threw another egg against the house. Another and another until the house was smeared with yoke and shell. My grandmother stared hard. I felt like crying.

"Leave her alone," I said. "You're scaring her."

Clara laughed. "That's the point."

Finally, my grandmother dropped the grocery bag and fled. I watched her disappear around the side of the house. Groceries tumbled out over the driveway.

"Clara," Tom said. "That wasn't necessary."

"It worked, didn't it?"

"You're a monster," I said to Clara. "I trusted you."

"No," Tom said. "She's a ghost. Just a ghost. And so are you."

"You're wrong. I know you're wrong." I picked up one of the items that had fallen from my grandmother's bag: an apple. Green, like the apple Tom had rolled to me in the cafeteria. A Granny Smith. As Tom and Clara watched, I turned it and took a huge bite. I swallowed roughly, the apple stuck in my throat. "I can get hungry," I said. "I can get thirsty. That means I'm not dead, right? You said you couldn't do that. I can sleep. I can feel cold and warmth. My heart beats. I'm breathing. I bleed. I ..." I saw a stick on the driveway, one of the many limbs that had fallen around the yard. "I can feel pain," I said. I dropped the apple and picked up the stick.

It was sharp and curved on the end, like a hook.

"Ez," Tom said.

In one quick motion, I cut my arm. Blood screamed across the skin. I winced in pain, and Clara gasped, but Tom moved toward me. He took the stick, broke it in half, and tossed it.

I gritted my teeth. "I can bleed," I said. "Can you do that? Can you bleed, Tom? I'm alive."

In the little bathroom off my bedroom, Martha the maid found gauze and bandages. I sat on the side of the rusted tub while she crouched before me, dabbing iodine on my arm.

I saw my arm. She saw it. She touched it. How could it not be real? How could I not be? What was happening to me? I felt pain from the cut, stinging from the antiseptic. But mostly what I felt was numbness; I was a doll Martha patted and tended. I was hollow. I didn't understand what was happening. No, none of this could be happening.

"Clara is a strange one," Martha was saying.

"I thought she was my friend," I said blankly.

"She's changeable. What she's been through and at her age, getting stuck at that age—well, I should have warned you. But Tom is kind. They will make good friends for you, keep you good company now that you're...." She stopped.

"I'm not dead, Martha," I said. "You can see my blood. You can feel my pulse."

Martha looked away, down at her work. I watched her doctor my arm. She wore a long dress and black leather shoes like Clara's, only they looked even older and more uncomfortable. She smelled strongly of laundry soap, something harsh and toxic, and of earth. I remembered Clara had smelled of earth too. Like a basement. Like a grave.

Martha unwrapped a bandage and pressed it on my arm. Her touch was warm, as Tom's had been.

"You *feel* alive," I said.

She shook her head. "But I'm not."

"How do you know?"

She held my fingers to her chest. "No ticking."

It was startling to lay my hand against a body that was not beating. Her collarbone felt solid, but there was no heartbeat beneath it, no movement, no comforting thrum.

"How did you figure it all out?" I whispered.

"When no one spoke to me. When no one seemed to see me or hear me. After awhile, then you know. You learn."

"I don't think I can believe this," I said. "I don't think this is real. Maybe I'm asleep. Maybe I'm still dreaming."

"Of course," Martha said. She squeezed my hand and I dropped it. "No one prepared you. But this house used to be full of people, children, generations of families—I watched them grow up. But no one ever saw me except the Builder, Mr. Black, Tom and Clara."

"The Builder?" I asked.

"You'll meet him. He built this house—and it took him."

"What do you mean, *it took him*?"

"He died here, Miss."

"What is this place, a death trap? Did the house kill you too?"

"Oh no, Miss," Martha said. "I did that."

I flinched as if I had been hit. This sweet girl, barely older than me. What had she done? What had happened? "How?" I said. "Why?"

She shook her head. "Not today. That's a story for another time, when you're feeling better." She put the iodine and gauze away in the medicine cabinet. "It won't last." She nodded at my arm. "The bandage, the work I did. It'll be undone by tomorrow at the latest, so you'll have to watch it. Re-bandage it yourself, now you know how."

I looked down at the bandage. It seemed secure to me. "Why won't it last?"

"Because I'm a ghost, of course, silly." She glanced out the window beside the sink. "That'll be Mr. Black out there now."

I rose and stood beside her. The strange man I had seen in the driveway was pacing in front of the barn, hands in his pockets, and kicking stones. He seemed to be talking to himself.

"He'll be wanting to go down to the pond again," Martha said. "But don't you let him."

"Why?" I asked.

"It's not good to re-visit the place of your death."

I felt sickness rising up in my throat. It was too much. It was all too much. I turned away from the window too sharply. The room spun. But a hand was there, a hand at my elbow, lowering me to the side of the tub. Not Martha's hand.

He had appeared so fast. "Do you feel all right?" Tom asked.

"Yes," I said. "Thanks to Martha."

She curtsied and left.

Tom sat on the edge of the tub beside me. "I'm sorry about Clara. She means well. It's just, we don't know how to do this. We've never met anyone like you before."

"Like what?"

"Someone who can interact with us; someone who is just like us, except, I suppose—"

"Not dead?"

"Right," he said.

"So you believe me."

"I think so." He sounded like he was talking himself into it. "The eating. The breathing. The bleeding. You're still cut, right? You still have a wound?"

I looked down at my bandage. "Pretty sure."

"I believe you. And you believe me?"

44

I looked at Tom. He wasn't what I had imagined a ghost would be like. But I had never really *thought* about ghosts too much before. I didn't want there to be a middle, a limbo, a world of ghosts. I didn't want there to be a halfway between the living and the dead. I didn't want it to be true, what he said he was.

I had a horrible thought. "Tom, my grandmother isn't dead, is she?"

He shook his head. "No. But she doesn't seem to be able to see or hear you, and neither does anyone else in this town except us. Did something happen to you before you came here? Something bad? Were you hurt?"

"I got in trouble," I said. "I hit my head."

"You hit your head?"

"I didn't die, Tom. I didn't hit it that hard. I was in a train tunnel. But I was pulled out—*alive*—and I got in big trouble. I wouldn't get threatened with jail time if I were dead, would I?"

"Probably not."

"Do you think hitting my head did ... something to me?"

He touched my arm, above the bandage. "*Something* happened to you."

When he touched me, I was surprised to feel what I had felt before when he had held my hand: a feeling of urgency. His touch was light and elusive, like something that might blow away, be taken from me. His hand felt not quite real. "Tom," I said. "In China, they treat strangers like ghosts."

"What do you mean?"

"My great-grandparents both emigrated. My grandma was the first to be born in this country. And in China, before you know a stranger, it's like she's not even there. Like she's a ghost to you. I thought my grandmother was doing that

45

to me. I thought she was mad at me, that I had offended her somehow. We didn't have ..." My voice trailed off. "It was hard with her before. She was really sad about my mom, and I don't think she wanted two little kids around, suddenly. And then we left. We never visited. My sister took me away. We barely even called. I thought I was a ghost to my grandmother. And it's like I *am* now, Tom. My sister hears me, but my grandmother can't."

Tom looked down at his hands. They were raggedy, the nails short and torn and dirty. Black with earth. He spoke into them, avoiding my eyes. "We think your grandmother might ... *notice* things sometimes."

"Notice things? What things?"

"The work Martha does around the house. Martha thinks your grandmother knows about it, appreciates it. Maybe Martha just needs her to."

I thought of the girl, not much older than me, who had taken care of me, the girl who had apparently made my bed and cleaned my room without me even knowing she was there because her work kept disappearing. "What happened to Martha?" I asked.

Tom stood. "That's a story for her to tell you."

I looked up at him. I knew I might be ending the conversation. But I had to ask it. I had to know. "What happened to *you*, Tom? How did you die? What killed you, Tom?"

But he wouldn't tell me.

CHAPTER 5

Death Beginning

I'm not sure what was harder to believe: that no one could see me except my new friends—or that all of my new friends were dead.

I didn't want to scare my grandmother, not like Clara had done with the eggs, but I hung around her, following her into rooms and lingering near doorways. I barely dared to speak to her, beyond calling her name. I had no idea what to say, how to even start to explain what was happening (what *was* happening?). Still, the evening that I hurt my arm, I tried.

I wrote her a letter.

I ripped a sheet of paper from a school notebook and found a pen. I sat cross-legged on my bed. *Dear Grandma,* I began. *I'm here but something's the matter. I'm sick or I'm ...* I couldn't finish the next thought. I didn't know what I was going to say, what excuse I was going to try to give.

But it didn't matter. Because the words faded. They disappeared.

I shook the pen. I dug through my bag and found another. That one didn't work either. Another pen, another. I tried a pencil. It wasn't the ink, I realized. It wasn't the lead.

It was me. I wasn't going to be able to get the words out. Even if my grandmother had owned a computer and I could have typed her letter, I knew somehow it wouldn't have worked. I couldn't make myself be seen.

And I couldn't make myself be heard. Or read.

I was trapped. Something had snared me. I willed my grandmother to notice me, just notice me, sense me. I waited for her to turn around, to turn off the TV, to see me.

She never did.

"I wanted that too," Clara said, simply. We were sitting at the end of the driveway, in the grass by the mailbox. "I thought if I just shouted," Clara said, "if I just made my voice loud enough, if I screamed."

"It didn't work?" I asked.

"I just screamed myself hoarse. I can make objects seem to float, and that's entertaining, but no one sees my hand holding the candlestick."

I looked away, down the road. Clara made me uncomfortable, but I couldn't seem to shake her; she could appear and disappear where she liked. "Where's Tom today?"

She shrugged. "He had a hard night last night."

"How can you have a hard night? You don't sleep. What do you do all the time?"

Clara stood. "There are ways of entertaining oneself. Like this." She nodded toward the road. "Here he comes. Just like I told you."

The truck pulled to a halt in front of the mailbox. In the front seat, a man in glasses sorted through a stack of envelopes. I felt nervous, like I was about to get in trouble, about to get caught. I didn't really trust Clara. But Clara said I *couldn't* get caught.

She pushed me forward and I tripped against the truck, grasping at the open window frame to steady myself. The man in the truck—the mail carrier—didn't notice. I said hello. He didn't notice.

I stood right beside the truck. I took the letters when he stretched them toward the mailbox. I was shaking so hard, I knocked them out of his hands.

He looked up, but not at me. He looked past me, right through me. He didn't retrieve the mail that had fallen. He didn't even get out of his truck. "Haunted house!" he said, and yanked the truck into reverse, moving away from us, as fast as he could.

I watched the truck careen down the road, then I picked up the mail from the mud.

"Good work," Clara said. "Now you know the post office can't see you. Oh well for your pen pals."

"You don't have to be so mean, Clara," a voice said—and Tom was there, at my side in the way that he and his sister and Martha had, appearing without warning.

I turned to him, and my smile at hearing his voice fell away. On his face, there was a bruise, a huge purple circle blackening his eye, bleeding darkly onto his skin.

Tom said it didn't hurt, but he wouldn't let me touch his face, or get an ice pack.

Or Martha. "It'll fade," he said. "I promise it will."

"I don't understand," I said. "I thought you couldn't bleed. I thought you couldn't get hurt, couldn't get bruised. I thought that's how you knew I wasn't dead."

"We can't get hurt," Clara said. "Unless—"

"Clara," Tom said.

She shrugged and turned, skipping back up the hill to the house.

"Tell me about the mailman," Tom said.

I couldn't look at Tom with his bruised eye. I looked at the ground instead. "He didn't see me. He cursed and ran away, said my grandmother's house was haunted. Do people know, about you and Clara and Martha? Does everyone in town know?"

"I don't know. There have been stories about this house for a long time. People say it's cursed."

"Did you live here? Was Martha your maid?"

"Oh no. We lived down the hill." He turned and pointed across the road, to an empty field. "There was a little shack there, by the railroad tracks. It was torn down, years and years ago. We had a view of the mansion on the hill, and at night, Clara and I talked about what it might be like to live there. But we didn't see anything or hear anything strange around the house before ..."

"Before you died."

"Yes." He faced me. "Is this too much for you?"

"That you're dead, or that you're talking to me? Or that I'm invisible? Or what?"

"All of it." He took my hand. His touch was warm. His hand was warm.

Real, I thought. *Alive.*

This was happening. We couldn't be figments or shadows or fades. We were real, and when he brought my face closer to his—that was real. And the fluttering in my stomach—that was real too. I felt true things. Everything was real except his breathing, which I couldn't hear; a pulse in his wrist, which I would never find; a heart, which could never beat for anyone.

"Your bruise," I said. The mark was already starting to fade. "What happened?"

"That must be nice." A man stood at the top of the driveway, the man in black with his hands in his pockets and sticking-up black hair. "Ghostie love," Mr. Black said.

I pulled away from Tom. "I'm not a ghost."

"Isn't it convenient, Tom, that a girl your age should die, just—what? A hundred or so years after your interment? Lucky you. You hardly waited at all."

A hundred years?

"Esmé Wong," Tom said. "Mr. Dylan Black. He's a decent friend, when he isn't tanked up."

Mr. Black made a little flourish with his hand, and attempted a bow, nearly tripping. He smelled—like earth, as Tom and Clara and Martha did—and like something else too, something strong, medicinal.

Alcohol. Mr. Black was drunk.

But that wasn't what worried me. "How old are you?" I asked Tom.

"Don't scare her off now," Mr. Black interrupted.

"When did you die?"

"Always an awkward question," Mr. Black said.

"Tom," I said.

He glanced at Mr. Black. "Isn't there a hay loft that needs haunting?"

Mr. Black shuffled away, muttering. Tom waited until he had gone. When he turned back to me, his eyes were flashing. How could they do that? How could they change depth, and sparkle, and lighten and darken? How could he be so changeable? He was dead.

"When?" I asked. "When did you die?"

"Ez," Tom said.

51

"If you won't tell me *how*, at least tell me *when*. At least tell me how old you are."

Tom said, not looking at me, "I died in 1903. I was seventeen."

"You've been seventeen for over a hundred years?"

"It's not that bad. It goes by quickly. You find things to do."

"What? I scared the mail carrier today. That took two minutes. What else have you been doing?"

"Trying to find a reason."

"A reason for what?" I said. Then I knew. His bruise was gone, had completely disappeared in the time we had been arguing, had healed itself—and his eyes had dulled too, hardening to a cold steel color. "Why are you haunting here?" I asked. "Is that it? Why are you a ghost, and not buried somewhere?"

"I am buried somewhere. Clara and I are next to each other. But no, I don't know why I'm a ghost. I don't know why I'm still here. I don't know what I'm supposed to be doing. None of us do. I've been trying to figure that out for over a hundred years."

"Who hit you?" I asked, staring at his eye, where the bruise had been. The skin there looked normal now. How could it heal so fast? How could the dead heal?

"Come with me," Tom said.

Beyond the pond, hills rose above the cow pasture. On top of the first hill grew a few bent trees. The hill had a large amount of jagged stones, the overgrown grass brushing up to my knees.

"What are we looking at?" I asked.

"Look down."

"So?" I said. "Rocks. No one mows here."

"Look closer."

I humored him, bending down to brush the weeds away from one of the stones. There were letters engraved on its surface. I shot up.

"It's not mine!" Tom said quickly. "It's the family plot."

"Could use a bit of tending," a mournful voice said and I looked behind me to see Mr. Black perched on a tilting gravestone, swinging his legs. "Your grandmother has almost forgotten the plot is here," he said. "Perhaps she doesn't want to remember. Upkeep really isn't her specialty, anyway, is it?"

"Aren't you supposed to be in the hayloft?" I asked.

He held up a flat green bottle, which sloshed when he shook it. "I had some hidden about here."

"Wait," I said. "I thought ghosts couldn't drink or eat?"

"We can," Tom said. "It just doesn't do anything. It doesn't taste like anything. It doesn't make us feel full or less thirsty or satisfied. We're never satisfied."

"And yet," Mr. Black said, swigging from the bottle, "we do what we know, what's familiar to us, what feels comforting. What we were doing when … well, you know."

"You were drunk when you died?"

"I was," Mr. Black said.

"So you're drunk forever. You're drunk as a ghost." I wrinkled my nose. "That's disgusting."

Mr. Black lifted the bottle and drank.

"His grave is over there," Tom said, pointing.

"You were family?"

"No," Mr. Black said. "But the family was a kind one, and arranged for some of their favorite servants to be buried here. I was the gardener."

"Martha's buried here, too," Tom said. "Beneath this tree."

I found her small stone, the letters caked with black moss. "*Martha Mary Moore,*" I read. "*Devoted and Faithful. November 14, 1881—January 1, 1900.* She was just nineteen. And she died on New Year's Day."

"New Year's Eve, actually," Mr. Black corrected. "But they didn't find her until the next morning."

"How do you know?"

"Why do you think I started drinking?" He took another sip, grimacing at the harsh taste. He got no pleasure from it, I saw. He drank like it was medicine.

I walked in a circle around the graveyard. It was like wading through deep water, the grass was so thick. "Who are all these people?" I said. "The others buried here? Why haven't I met them? Why aren't *they* ghosts? Why isn't the house full of ghosts?"

"I don't know," Tom said. "It's just me and Clara and Mr. Black."

"And Martha," Mr. Black said.

"And the Builder," Tom said.

"And—"

Tom looked at him sharply, and he drank.

"Why haven't I met the Builder?" I asked. "Where is he?"

"Building, I imagine," Mr. Black said. "Putting in some cupola, or a stairway that leads to nowhere."

"He keeps busy," Tom said. "He does what he knows. He built this house. And he keeps on building it."

I gazed down at the house at the bottom of the field: the stained-glass fanlight above the doors, the boxy addition on the back. The house had been added onto over the years, and some pieces matched more than others. "Where are you buried?" I asked Tom.

He opened his mouth to speak, but his words were drowned out by a sound: a horn, blaring and close.

"The train," Mr. Black said when the blast had ended.

"I came into town on that train," I said.

Tom said, "Me too." And then he began to run.

"Stop him!" Mr. Black said. He leapt from the headstone, the bottle crashing to the ground and breaking. Mr. Black didn't even glance at it. "Go after him!"

But Tom was gone, halfway past the house already.

"What's the matter with you?" I said. "Where's he going?"

Mr. Black bounded through the weeds and extended his hand to me. Without even thinking, I took it and we ran down the hill, past the house, over the driveway and across the road. It was the first time I had run with a ghost. We didn't fly, not exactly, but we seemed to reach the train station in the time it took me to blink, to breathe in and out. I think my feet touched the ground only twice, like a send-off, a moon-bounce. I felt Mr. Black's hand, hard and strong, in my own. His black scarf flapped in the wind. Then we were on the platform outside the train station, Mr. Black resting with his arm against the wall; running with me appeared to have exhausted him.

"Where's Tom?" I asked.

Mr. Black just pointed at the tracks. He seemed breathless, though he had no breath.

I crept to the edge of the platform, and saw Tom down below, stepping over the rails. Silver flashed in his hands. It was a wrench. "Tom, what are you doing?" I said.

He looked up at me briefly, then bent back to his work. He was twisting at something, trying to turn a lever on the ground. He didn't seem to see me. No, he didn't seem to *know* me.

A light sped toward the tracks, blinding even in daytime. The train, the Keystone. The Keystone was coming. I glanced back at Mr. Black, then hopped down from the platform. I landed on my feet, shaky but standing. "Tom, what are you doing?" I repeated. I reached him and tried to touch him, grabbing for the wrench, but he yanked it back.

"Stopping the train." His hands kept moving. "Changing its path. I have to do this."

"Why? Is there someone on the train? Tom, it's a real train. There are *people* on it. Innocent living people."

He looked at me. His face had more color. It was dirty, I realized, and through the dirt snaked pale, silvery tears. Tom was crying. "Living people matter more than me?"

"No," I said. "I don't know."

The train blasted its horn. The conductor couldn't have seen us; no one saw us. It was just what the train did automatically when it approached a station. But the sound was so close, I felt it in my chest, felt it coming through the ground: the deep resonate bass of the engine. The train cleared the curve right before the station.

"*Tom,*" I said.

"Well, ho there." Walking to us, picking his way across the tracks, swinging a lantern, was a man.

I felt arms. I felt myself being lifted. I felt weightless, my body pulled up and away from the tracks, the headlight, the roaring engine. I saw the man who had spoken was an old man.

I was dead. I had died in the subway tunnel in New York, and now I was repeating my death. Now I would do it again and again: hit my head, see the darkness; the worker would pull my body of out the tunnel.

So this was what being dead was like. I was floating above the scene, watching Tom and the old man with the lantern getting smaller. As I left the station behind, I saw the man look up at me. He wore a rumpled brown hat. His face was thin and gristly, his chin spotted with white. He smiled, but it was a cold smile. Sunlight glittered against his teeth. It made me shiver.

I smelled alcohol. I turned my face and met Mr. Black's dark and smelly shirt. He was holding me, running with me. I pushed at him, but he held tight. "What are you doing?"

"Saving your life," he said. "If you *are* alive, as everyone says you are, you should stay that way, I guess."

"But Tom's back there."

His jaw tensed. "Can't be helped."

"A train is coming."

"He won't stop it. He never does." Mr. Black carried me in through the sloping doors of the barn, and up a ladder. He didn't stop until we were in the hayloft, and he set me down on a mound of straw.

"What's going on?" I said.

"Stay here," he said. "Be quiet."

"Why?"

"Shh. For once." He held up his hand, and I listened. At first I heard nothing, just the chatter of birds, pigeons or doves. The barn roof had so many holes, light filtered through, spotting my hands and Mr. Black's face. Then I heard a horn, fainter now.

Mr. Black relaxed. "The train's left. It's over."

"What is? What's going on?"

He was rustling around in the straw. He got on his hands and knees and moved away from me, searching in the shadows.

"What about Tom?" I asked.

"Tom is dead. Now, where did I put that …?"

"What happened to him just now? Why did he act that way? Who was that man?"

"Ah!" Mr. Black lifted a bottle from the hay, brushed away the dust, and uncorked it with his teeth. "That was Tom's death." He spit the cork into the shadows. "You saw him die again, saw the start of it, anyway. You saw his death beginning."

"And who was that man? That old man with the lantern?"

Mr. Black drank long and deep before answering. "That was the man who killed him."

CHAPTER 6

Sensitive One

I didn't see Tom for days.

I was learning another thing about ghosts: they could make themselves scarce when they wanted to, and now, they wanted to. Or Tom did, anyway.

I tried to develop a routine. I did everything I would normally do, but I attempted to be more careful about it. I ate only when my grandmother was gone, and I always washed and dried my dishes and put them back in the cabinets right away. I knew I would terrify her—an invisible granddaughter—and what could she do about it, anyway? I didn't know what to say to her; I had barely had anything to say to her when I *was* visible.

Martha helped, in her way. It made me uncomfortable, all the work she did for no reason, but I could never catch her, never see her tucking in the sheets, or cleaning the bathroom, or dusting the dozens of rooms. The sheets always un-tucked themselves by bedtime, and the rust stubbornly returned to the tub, but I could see why my grandmother thought I wasn't there.

Sometimes I wasn't sure myself.

Martha covered my tracks in the house, and my sister? She just couldn't hear what I was saying, couldn't understand.

"I understand," she said automatically. "You feel invisible."

"No," I insisted. "I am invisible. I *am*."

"Grandma is very busy and you have opposite schedules, but you need to have a conversation with her. Have you really even talked with her yet?"

"I *can't*!" I said. "Can I please come home?"

"We'll talk about that later, okay? But for right now, this is your home, Esmé. This is where you live."

But I felt barely alive.

One thing was certain: I was not going back to that school. Not if no one noticed. Not if I wasn't even getting credit.

"Oh come now," Martha said, scanning the closet in my room. She had unpacked my suitcases one night while I slept (though I had to re-unpack them). She had put away my clothes, and now she took them out, one by one, appraising the T-shirts and jeans she had ironed and folded and hung on hangers. Multiple times. She shook her head, and put the clothes back on the rack. "School is important," Martha said. "School will get you a better life."

"One where I'm not invisible?" I said.

"You can learn a lot, being invisible," Martha said, disappearing into the closet again.

"Like what?"

"How to speak, how to act. Certain people's secrets."

I sat up on the bed, watching her. "Secrets?" I said. "Like, what secrets?"

"Servants are supposed to be invisible. We have separate stairs, separate entrances, separate living quarters."

"What secrets, Martha?"

She came out of the closet, holding a yellow dress. "Now, why don't you ever wear something nice like this?"

I groaned. "I hate dresses. My sister must have packed that."

"No one can see you, anyway. Why not wear a dress like a regular lady?"

"Because I'm not a regular lady. Martha, come on." I pulled a tasseled pillow to my chest. "What secrets do you know? Tell me. What do you know about my grandmother?"

She sat on the edge of the bed, the yellow dress in her lap. "Not very much," she admitted, "even after all these years. Your grandmother keeps to herself. She leaves at night. She works."

"At a nursing home. She's a nurse."

"And she has nurse things," Martha agreed. "Hot water bottles and medicine and needles and such. But she also has ..." She leaned forward so I did too, "other objects."

"What do you mean?"

"Cards," Martha said solemnly.

"Cards?"

Martha sat back with a satisfied nod.

"Playing cards? Prescription cards?"

"Cards with horrible pictures on them—weeping women, skulls on fire, men with swords. Cards that tell the future, Clara says."

I thought. "Tarot cards?"

"Perhaps. Perhaps that's what they're called." Martha brushed an invisible speck of dust off her apron. "Nothing good about them, that's all I know. Not good medicine."

"Martha, kids at school—I overheard them talking. One of them said my grandmother was a witch. Do you know anything about that?"

Martha stood up from the bed, shaking out the folds of the yellow dress. "There's no truth to it. Your grandmother is a good woman. People in town tell stories, it's true. But there have been stories about this house forever. Those stories don't concern your grandmother, don't have nothing to do with her. She's an innocent old woman." She frowned slightly. "Except for the cards."

I thought of how my grandmother had seemed the first night I had arrived in Wellstone, when she didn't see me, couldn't see me, when she had returned home alone. I had walked in on her in the big empty house, by herself in the sitting room, watching the TV on mute. *Lonely*, is what I had thought. I thought I had understood.

"Martha," I said. "Is there another ghost here?"

Martha was hanging up the dress. "Hmm?"

"Other than the four of you, and the Builder, I mean. Is there a man maybe? An old man? Another ghost who hangs around the train station? Mr. Black said Tom was ... Mr. Black said this old man at the train station *hurt* Tom. Did he push him in front of the train? I thought I remembered ghost stories about an old man in Wellstone. Did the train hit the man too, or—"

Martha came out of the shadows. "Don't worry about Tom's death, Miss. It's over now. It's over and done."

But it wasn't.

I rode the bus to school. I shuffled along with the rest of the students, but I didn't go to class. Any class. After the late bell, I could make my way through the halls without fighting, squeezing against the wall to avoid being stepped on, run into, or tripped over. I found the library.

It was windowless, cool, and empty. Rows of computers stretched out before the door and the circulation desk where the librarian sat, clicking on another keyboard. I chose a computer away from the door, with a screen not facing the librarian, thinking that if a student came in, he wouldn't walk this far just to check email.

But someone did come in and stand behind me. Clara.

I felt uneasiness whenever she showed up now, like something might explode or go missing. I tried to concentrate on the screen. "Where's Tom?" I said without looking at her.

"Don't know," Clara said. "Avoiding you."

I stopped typing. "Why?"

"You embarrassed him. You saw his death."

"I didn't," I said.

"You came close."

I twisted in the chair. "Clara, he just took off in the middle of talking to me. He heard the train and was gone. I had no idea what was happening. If he was hit by a train, if that's how ..." I couldn't make myself say it. "How *it* happened, other people would have seen his death too. Anyone on the platform or train would have seen."

"He wasn't hit by a train," Clara said. "Shows how much you know. That's not how he died. That's not at all how it happened."

"Tell me how then."

But she bent down to the computer, her fingers outstretched. "Oh, the magic box! Tom doesn't like them, but I do. You can make it sing. You can look at dancing hamsters. Students do it all the time."

"Clara." I put my hands over the keyboard, blocking her. "I'm doing something important, okay?"

I waited until she had left, then I opened a browser, and tried not to think about Tom.

There were over a million search results for *invisible*. Invisible ink, invisible fencing, a rumor about invisible paint. A faerie tale: twelve princesses who made themselves invisible every night so that they could sneak away from their room and dance. And then a boy followed them, found them out, snapped a twig from each magical tree they passed on their way to the underworld of dancing: a gold tree, a silver one.

"Great," I said. "All I need is some boy to follow me and break off a magical branch."

I hadn't realized I had spoken out loud. But the library student aide, a small girl with frizzy hair, spilled a cup of pencils across the circulation desk.

Had she heard me?

I stood up from the computer. I thought she looked at my chair as it pushed away from the table. Maybe, just maybe, I wasn't invisible anymore. Maybe it had ended, whatever it was that had happened to me. "Hello?" I said.

She looked around. "Miss Simms?" The girl had braces. Invisible braces.

I waved. "Hello? I'm right in front of you. Can you see me? Can you really see me?"

"Miss Simms?" the girl said again. She looked through me, wouldn't—or couldn't—make eye contact with me. "There's something wrong with one of the computers." She vaulted up the stairs to the second story, where the librarian had disappeared ages ago.

I slumped back down in the chair.

"A sensitive one," Tom said. "Sometimes they can sense something—even hear you if it's quiet enough." He stood beside me.

I was too disappointed to be relieved he was back. I thought the girl had seen me. I thought maybe... but no.

"Stop doing that," I said to Tom. "Stop sneaking up on me. I know you don't have footsteps—I guess you don't—but it drives me crazy."

I wanted to touch him, to reach out and make sure it was really him, to convince myself. I didn't know if he was okay, if a ghost could be okay or not. I didn't know what to say to him. He had held my hand. But he had also screamed at me without seeing me, blinded by tears. He had tried to derail a train.

I took a breath. "Are you all right?"

"Fine." He shrugged. "Dead."

"What happened back there at the train station?"

His eyes didn't leave mine, but his face turned hard. "I would prefer not to talk about that."

"I get that," I said.

"What did you find out?"

I glanced back at the computer. Was I just going to let it go, let him change the subject? This time I was. "Not very much about invisibility," I said. "Nothing about the subway. No one reports turning invisible after being underground. I thought it might be a chemical, maybe. Maybe something was wrong with the paint that was spilled there, or there was some kind of secret experiment going on? But I don't think so. A lot of people seem to *want* to be invisible, according to the internet."

Tom glanced around. "Let's get out of here. It's almost the class change, and there's a class in here next period."

We exited the library just as the bell rang, students flooding the halls. I winced, but Tom kept walking calmly, unchanged, making a path for me down the middle of the hall. He held onto my arm. And no one ran into us.

"How do you do that?" I asked.

"Practice."

I felt something brush against my hand. "I guess I still need to work on my technique," I said. But then the brush became a tug, a pinch. "Ouch," I said. I looked down.

A girl stood beside me. She had washed-out blond hair falling from a center part, deep gray circles under her eyes. She clutched a stack of books. And she was looking straight at me. "Excuse me?" she said. "Can you help me? I can't find my locker."

I turned around, searching for the person she must have been addressing.

But she touched me again, yanking on the hem of my yellow dress, the one Martha had made me wear.

The girl touched me. She saw me. Invisible me.

"Me?" I said. "You see me? You're talking to me?"

"Help me," she said. "I need to find my locker."

"Seriously?" I said. I was almost excited. "You do?"

But I felt myself being pulled in another direction.

Tom had grabbed my arm. He was sprinting with me, as Mr. Black had done. By the time I opened my mouth to protest, we had gone down the hall, far away from the girl. There were students in between us, jostling and hurrying to class, hiding us from her.

"What are you doing?" I said. "She saw me. She actually talked to me. We have to go after her. Either I'm no longer invisible—or she's a sensitive one, or whatever."

"She isn't sensitive."

"Maybe she can help us."

"No," Tom said flatly. "She can't."

"Why?" I asked.

"Because she's a ghost."

I remembered the girl's face, pale as if she had been drained of blood, the circles under her eyes. "Well, we have to help her then."

"No."

I stared at him. "Tom, you helped me. When you and Clara thought I was a ghost, you were going to help me. You were going to go out of your way to make me understand. We have to make her understand."

"She understands," Tom said.

"I don't think she does."

Then I heard a roar. The students scattered, clearing a circle in the center of the hall. In the middle of the circle, a boy lay on his side, books tossed around him. His face looked stunned, slack and hurt. There was a minute of silence when no one moved. Then the moment passed, tension broke. The students began to laugh and talk and move again, to help the boy up, to walk around him.

"Way to trip," one of them said.

But the boy *hadn't* tripped on his own.

He had been made to fall by the blond girl, by the ghost— and I had seen it. I had seen her move, a flash through the crowd as she terrified him. I had seen her mouth drop open, heard the keening sound that escaped. The roar, the inhuman roar of pain and anguish. It had happened in a blink, but I had seen it, seen her target him.

"Why did she do that?" I whispered. "Why did she scare him?"

"I don't know," Tom said. "But she doesn't need us. She knows she's dead—and she's angry about it. She wants to hurt other people like she was hurt."

The boy limped off, supported by friends. Blood leaked from his nose onto his shirt.

Tom and I went to the cafeteria, and sat down at a center table. People gave us space without even knowing they were doing it. It was like being in bubble, like how the Firecracker said strangers treated famous people in the city, pretending the celebrities weren't there, pretending they didn't see them while also accommodating them.

No one had to pretend not to see or hear us. It made carrying on a secret conversation easy.

"Tell me about the ghost girl," I said. "Do you know her? Do all ghosts know each other?"

"No," Tom said. "But I know her type. She's a malicious spirit."

"What's that?"

"That kind of ghost that would try to get you to harm yourself."

I scanned the cafeteria. All around us, students laughed and ate and stood in line. They looked so happy, innocent. Had I ever looked like one of them, been one of them? Everything they did—all their lives—had to be easy. They were visible; they were alive.

"She's not here anymore," Tom said. "I don't sense her. Do you?"

"I guess not."

He peered down the empty table. "Are you hungry? Would you like to eat something? I can filch you an apple. I used to be good at that."

"Tom," I said, "what was your life like before?"

He made a face that was half grimace, half smile. "Not good."

"Why did you go back to the train tracks? Martha said it's not right to go back to the place of your death. She said you're not supposed to. And Mr. Black tried to stop you. Why did you do it?"

He wouldn't meet my eyes. "I feel like I have something to do. I can't explain it. Clara doesn't feel it so strongly, but

I do. And the only thing I can think of is the worst thing that ever happened to me."

"Dying?"

"No," he said. "My *father*." He spit the word.

I remembered the man at the train station: the old man with the lantern, his hat, his greasy grin. "That man on the tracks was your father?"

"Adopted. He adopted us. He wanted us to call him *Papa*, but we wouldn't. He didn't act like one."

No one was looking at us. No one ran into us, or brushed past us, or bumped us, though we sat in the center of everything. And now it seemed like I couldn't see the other students either, like I couldn't even hear them. All the noise and talking and laughter fell away. Everything was silence. Everything except us.

"He killed you," I said. "How?"

"He liked to hit. Funny thing about ghosts, Ez. We can't feel pain, can't feel temperatures, can't bleed or bruise— *except* when it comes to our own death. We can feel that, experience *that*, again and again, with just as much pain as the first time if we're not careful. And I'm not careful."

I remembered the bruise on his face, how quickly it had disappeared. Why hadn't I asked more questions? The words left my mouth before I could stop them. "I need you to be careful," I said.

It was then that I knew, knew for sure without a doubt, that something had happened to me and I was different, different beyond belief, that I was invisible, for good, for real, maybe forever. Because Tom Griffin kissed me in the middle of the high school cafeteria, in the midst of the lunch rush—and no one said a word.

CHAPTER 7

Riding Too Long

I asked Martha about Tom. There was so much I didn't know: hobbies, fears, dreams (did ghosts have dreams?). "Girls?" I asked. "Have there been girls?"

"No," Martha said. "Not that I know of, Miss, and I know just about everything that happens in this house. There have been other ghosts we've met along the years, but they don't last. They're just passing through, the other dead. They come and go. But Tom and his sister, Mr. Black, the Builder and me—for some reason, we're the ones who have stayed."

She was turning down my bed as she spoke, even though I had asked her not to. It was a comfort, Martha said, to do the familiar job, to do the job still, to make the house nice for someone, especially someone who noticed, someone who could thank her, which I did repeatedly, though it never seemed like enough.

"Does Tom ever talk about his father?" I asked.

"No. And don't go calling him that. He was no father."

"What should I call him then?"

"Nothing. Don't talk about him. Don't say his name. It upsets Tom."

"But I want to help."

Martha patted the bed. "Say your prayers now."

"I don't say prayers, Martha."

She closed her eyes. "I wish your grandmother was a ghost so she could see to properly raising you."

I slipped under the covers, doing my best not to mess up the smooth tucked envelope Martha had made of the sheets. I pulled the quilt up to my chin. "We kissed," I whispered. "Me and Tom."

Her hands flew up. She bounced onto the end of the bed. "What was it like?"

I was expecting her to be shocked or to scold me, maybe, not to be springing on the mattress. "What was what like?"

Martha glanced over her shoulder, then leaned down to me and whispered: "*Kissing.*"

"Martha, you've never been kissed before? You're nineteen."

"I know." Her hands fluttered to her face, covering the blush that might have appeared on the cheeks of a living girl. "I've never had the occasion."

"Why?"

"Well, I started work at fourteen. My first position was out in the country, no decent young men, all hayseeds there. I was eighteen when I came to work here at the house. And then ..."

"There were no men in Wellstone?"

"Not one that I wanted. Not one who wanted me." She stood up from the bed.

"Wait, wait!" I said. "Don't go yet." I felt like I had my sister back. "Don't you want me to tell you about kissing?"

But Martha said, "Maybe not tonight, Miss," and flicked off the light.

*

I dreamed of Tom. *Kissing* Tom.

Kissing a ghost.

I couldn't look at him. My lips were buzzing, my skin was on fire. His fingers grazed my cheekbones, and his touch was not cold, not at all. It was warm. It felt real. It *was* real. I had kissed a ghost. I had been kissed by a ghost, a boy technically a hundred years older than me. It was a good kiss, I thought. It was not my first. But it was the first where I felt like I wanted it, where I felt *something*, some feeling I couldn't yet name.

A sound outside woke me. Rising from the bed, I went to the window in time to see a figure run across the grass, his limbs glowing in the moonlight, his black hair blending into clouds.

Tom.

I dressed, tucking the long T-shirt I slept in into a pair of jeans, yanking on tennis shoes as I tripped downstairs. And then I was outside, running before my eyes had fully adjusted, hurtling myself into the shadows. The grass was dewy and slick, and I stumbled down the hill to the road. No cars. No streetlights, either. Tom fled down the hill ahead of me. He had almost disappeared.

Then I heard a whistle.

I didn't think I could run any faster—but I did. I ran until I couldn't feel my feet, or my long hair hitting my back. I ran as the terrain beneath me changed from asphalt to grass and back to concrete. I lost sight of Tom.

The train station was empty under the moon. A train cooled on the tracks, wheels steaming, and before it, on the rails, he lay.

I prepared myself to jump, to leap down to him. There was no other way onto the tracks. But Clara said, "It's too late."

She was there, of course she was there.

"I have to go to him," I said.

"It was too late decades ago." She grabbed my arm until I was face to face with her, her cold black eyes staring into mine. "Have you ever seen a dead body before?"

"Clara." I pulled away from her.

"Well, you won't see one today. Tom died years ago, all right? Years and years. That's not his body down there. It's his ghost. It's painful, but it's temporary, what he's done. He'll be back."

Out of the corner of my eye, there he was: a strange shape, so still on the tracks. I had never seen anyone be so still. "Why?" I asked. "Why does he do it? Why does he come back here, night after night, to die?"

"He seems to think he can stop it, stop being a ghost."

"Do you?"

"Not really. What's done is done. We died. We're ghosts. We might as well make the best of it." Her eyes darted. "Like kissing strangers. I suppose that's something we could do."

"You saw?" I said, weakly. Her eyes were so dark, and the rest of her colorless, bloodless. The contrast was alarming, as stark as ash on snow.

"You shouldn't have been flaunting it," Clara said.

"I wasn't—"

"You think you're so smart because you're alive, so special. You want to be with Tom," Clara said. "Fine. Be with Tom."

I saw her arms flare out, palms first, and come toward me. I backed up, and she pushed me. I stumbled backward over the lip of the platform, and fell, landing on my shoulder in the gravel beside the train tracks.

Clara towered above me. "You're not dead, Esmé. You're not one of us. You don't belong here, and you don't belong with Tom."

"I live here," I said. "*Live*. You're the one that doesn't belong." I struggled to a standing position. I was about to remind Clara that this was my home, but *Wellstone*? Home? What was wrong with me?

I rubbed my aching shoulder. Had it been only a few weeks? Weeks since I had gone to school in New York, since I had sat in the back of the classroom with Acid: a normal guy, who never called. I had been normal, seen. It seemed like years ago. I remembered the train…

The train stopped in Wellstone once a day—once only, in the afternoon. I remembered because the Firecracker had made a big deal about how I couldn't miss the train. We couldn't be late, because it was the only one. But it was midnight now, past midnight.

What was *this* train?

Clara had disappeared. I forced myself to look beyond Tom. *It's not him*, I told myself. *It's not him*.

I focused on the train behind him. The engine faced me, black and hulking. This was not like the train that had brought me from New York: a modern, streamlined train, with blue-and-silver cars. This train was smaller. There was a bronze bell on the engine, and a smokestack that leaked a gray plume.

The smoke drifted in front of the train, engulfing me. I gagged and coughed. Putting my arm over my eyes, I walked, half-blind, alongside the train. Behind the engine stretched a line of passenger cars. They were wooden, painted green. Their windows were closed.

And peering through every one of them was a face.

I backed away, right into the cloud of smoke. I coughed, choking, and the faces came alive behind the windows, moving and squirming. They had seen me. They were trying to shout at me. They were all children.

Children stared out of the windows, pressing against the glass. Their faces were gray as dirty sheets, so gray they looked almost purple, sick, with circles under their eyes. They opened their mouths, but no sound came out. They shut their mouths like fish: blankly, mute.

It looked like they were trying to scream.

I staggered away from the children, smoke searing my eyes. The passenger cars disappeared in the plume. I couldn't breathe, but a hand found my shoulder. Clara. Come to her senses, or come to fight me.

"Clara," I coughed. "What's wrong with this train?"

"Nothing wrong with it," a man said. "Except you've been riding too long."

The hand spun me around, clenched down on my shoulder, so tight it met bone. The smoke thinned and I saw him: the brown hat, the stubble, the gray, stinking teeth. It was the man from the train tracks, the man with the lantern.

Tom's father. Tom's killer.

He leered at me. His teeth were big and straight and stained. His hand was clamped firm on my shoulder, fingers digging into my flesh. "How many stops have you seen, child?" he asked me. "How many?"

"Clara!" I screamed.

"Got a mouth on her, that's good. Got a powerful set of lungs. Got some muscles to go with those lungs?" His hand moved down my arm, squeezing me.

I shook and twisted. "Get off me!"

But the man held tight. His other hand grabbed my jaw,

squeezing my mouth open as I tried to scream. And when his finger drifted into my mouth, feeling for teeth, I didn't hesitate.

I bit.

He yanked his hand out of my mouth, yelling. He lost his grip on my shoulder. I reared back and kicked him in the knees as hard as I could. He doubled over, and I ran, plunging into the smoke.

When the cloud cleared, I could see the platform ahead of me. My shoulder throbbed, but I lifted myself up, putting all my weight on my arms. I had swung one leg over the side of the platform when I felt it.

Pain. More pain.

Pain in my back. Pain tearing through my spine, delivered from a sharp blow in the center near my backbone. My hands slipped and I fell back onto the tracks and curled onto my side, groaning. The fall was hard, but it was nothing compared to the hurt between my shoulder blades. It was a hot pain, searing.

I had been burned.

I heard crunching gravel: footsteps. From where I lay, I could see two worn, brown work boots approaching. "Don't you walk away when I'm talking to you."

I didn't have the strength to raise my head.

Something landed in the gravel at the man's feet, inches from my face: a large, red metal object, handle swinging. I knew it was the thing that had hit me. The lantern. Flame burned at its core. I could feel the heat pulsing from the glass.

The lantern disappeared from view as the man picked it up again. I managed to lift my head off the ground in time to see him stand over me, raising the burning lantern above his head.

There was a splintering sound. Something sharp rained down upon me, and I covered my eyes with my arm. A thud, and I opened my eyes to see the man had fallen onto his side in the gravel. Broken glass trickled over his face.

On the platform, staring down at us, stood Martha and Mr. Black. Mr. Black held the jagged remains of a bottle.

"What now?" I whispered.

"Now," Mr. Black said, reaching down to me. "We run."

We ran to the house. We swung the big front doors shut behind us, the rusted hinges groaning after so long hanging open, and we stood behind them, peering out through the windows on both sides. I was breathing hard.

Mr. Black and Martha were not breathing at all.

"So ghosts can hurt each other," I said, "if they hurt each other in life. And ghosts can hurt me. Ghosts can hurt the living."

"Well, we didn't know that," Mr. Black said. "It's not as if we've done that before. What kind of ghosts do you take us for?"

"And," Martha exchanged a look with Mr. Black, "it's not as if you're exactly living."

"What does that mean?" I said.

"You're in between is all, Miss. Not dead, but not … seen."

"That man who killed Tom, do you think he'll follow us?"

"No," Mr. Black said. "He won't come in the house. Not allowed."

"Why?"

"He never lived here in life, and we're bound by our patterns. *I* shouldn't have even come in, not through the front doors, anyway."

Martha put her hand on his arm. "It's fine."

We all looked at her hand for a moment, resting on Mr. Black's dark sleeve. He stared at it, then at her. She took her hand away.

Mr. Black cleared his throat and continued. "Only allowed at the back door, and only to ask a question. Don't want to track mud in the house. Don't want to make a mess."

"Where did you sleep then?" I asked him.

"Above the stables."

"There's no one left to care anymore," Martha said. "Besides, your work is just as important as a house servant's. The garden used to be—"

"*Used* to be," Mr. Black said.

I turned away from them to look out the window again. The yard was dark, and all was silent, but I knew I couldn't go to bed. I would never be able to sleep now. "Who *was* that man?" I asked. "What was his name?"

"The Stationmaster," Martha said simply. "We don't know his name. He took Tom and Clara in when they were living, and he treated them no-good, and he deserved what came to him eventually."

"Which was what?"

"Killed by a train."

I shuddered. He was the man from the stories; the ghost in the woods, the one I had vaguely remembered; the reason children, when I had lived in Wellstone before, had been afraid to play beyond their own yards.

"Time to go to bed, Miss," Martha said. "If you can sleep, you should."

I shook my head. "I'll wait up for Tom, thanks."

"We can send him up to your room when he gets home," Mr. Black said.

Martha looked horrified. "No. We can't."

We compromised. Mr. Black brought in a dusty velvet chair from the sitting room for me. He placed it by the front doors, and I promised try and sleep. And even though the chair was uncomfortable, the ancient velvet crackling every time I shifted, I did fall asleep. Sometime in the night, someone—probably Martha—put an afghan over my shoulders. But later, something caused me to turn and wake.

My grandmother stood in the hall, staring at me.

She was dressed to go out, her hair curled at her chin. She wore a raincoat and carried her big black leather bag, a doctor's or nurse's bag, I thought, except a tall white candle poked out of one of the pockets. What was she doing? Was there an emergency at the nursing home? What kind of an emergency needed candles?

I was cold. The afghan, which had slipped off my legs, lay puddled on the floor. And my grandmother stood there, staring.

It must have been the chair. The chair was out of place. The afghan didn't belong on the floor. Grandmother had a big house, but surely she would remember that she hadn't left a chair here in the hallway.

Yet she wasn't staring at the chair, or at the closed doors, or at the afghan. She seemed to be looking into my eyes. She almost looked like she was listening for me.

"Grandma?" I said. "Grandma, it's me."

She tilted her head. Her eyes left mine and unfocused. But then she shook her head. Tightening her grip on her bag, she pulled her coat closed, and then she was gone through the doors. Soon I heard the sound of her car starting.

She had never said a word.

Tom came home at dawn. I woke up in gray light, and he was there, pulling the afghan, which had slipped down again, back over me. "It's just me," he said.

I looked for bruises on his face, but I couldn't see them in the dim hall. "Are you okay?" I asked.

"Still dead." He might have smiled.

But I didn't. "What's wrong with you? Why did you go back there *again*?"

The smile, if there was one, vanished. "One of these days, I'm going to change things. One of these days, I'll hurt *him*. You'll see, Ez. Except you won't. You won't be there. I don't want you there. I don't want you following me again, all right? It's not safe."

Something bubbled up in me. I shook off the blanket. "You can't control me," I said. "I'm alive. I'm invisible. I can go anywhere." I unfolded my legs from the chair, intending to rise, but pain shot through me.

"What's wrong? Did something happen?"

I rose from the chair with difficulty. "Ghosts can hurt me," I said. "Did you know that? Maybe because I'm invisible, Martha thinks. Not dead but not fully alive. You can hurt me, and you can ..." I wanted to say *kiss me*.

No, I wanted *him* to say it—and then to kiss me again.

But he didn't. "Who hurt you?" he asked. "The Stationmaster? Did he hit you?"

"Technically," I said, "he burned me."

"That's it. That's enough. Clara said this was wrong, and it is. It isn't fair to you. It isn't right."

"What isn't?"

"As soon as we knew, as soon as we found out you weren't a ghost, that you weren't one of us, we should have let you be. I should have. You're not dead. You still have a life to live. I can't let you be hurt by my death, my mistake."

"You're not *letting me* do anything," I said. "And being killed by a lantern-swinging psycho is not your mistake, you know. Not your fault. Unless you could have stopped him from being your dad."

Tom was silent for a moment. "I could have," he said. He turned from me. He could drift away in a heartbeat. He could choose to hide himself from me, for days, forever. He could appear in a moment. He could carry me as if we were flying.

I couldn't control him, but it was impossible to control anyone, even the living. So I just kept talking. "What was that train? The train from New York doesn't come through at night. That was a ghost train. That was a train from your time, wasn't it?"

"Something like that," he said.

"Was that train full of ghosts?"

"Yes."

"Why were they all children?"

He paused. "They were orphans."

CHAPTER 8

Wickedness and Snares

Black-and-white images swam up to the screen of the computer in the school library: photographs of children hanging out of train windows; a huge group gathered on the tracks around an engine, their faces thin and pinched. No one smiled.

Two hundred thousand, the computer said.

An estimated two hundred thousand children from New York and other cities were taken from their homes, put on trains, and shipped off to find new homes in the country. The trains would stop in small, rural towns, the children were placed on stages, and anyone who wanted to could take them home.

Anyone.

I read stories of happy families where children were adopted, lived on farms, grew healthy, loved. I read stories of children who became farmhands, or indentured servants. Or worse. Tom was one of those kids, I knew. I knew without him telling me that his story was one of the unhappy ones.

The trains were called baby trains and orphan trains, but some of the children weren't orphans at all. Some had one parent. Some children were poor, or had run away, or had parents who drank. Some children were working themselves out on the streets—selling newspapers or flowers, or stealing. Or worse.

During the class change, I ducked beneath the desk and hid. I saw the shoes of students entering and exiting the library. I heard books slapping on the counter and sliding through the book return.

Then a student stumbled; I saw the sneaker that tripped her. The student landed face down on the floor, scattering her books, and I recognized her. It was the library aide, the frizzy haired girl with braces who seemed to have heard me, who had sensed me. *Sensitive*, Tom had called her. A sensitive one.

And an unpopular one, it looked like.

There was laughing, and a boy's voice said, "What's the matter, spooky?"

"Check out a book on walking," another voice said. "Freak."

The sneakers turned and exited. Slowly, the library aide slid up to her knees. She was shaking as she collected her books. Without thinking, I reached out my hand. I only meant to help her, to pick up the books that had fallen under the desk, but she stiffened, eyes wide, as my invisible fingers brushed her elbow. I started to pull back, then I thought I might as well take advantage of my state.

"It's okay," I said softly. "It's going to be okay. One day you'll leave this town."

She re-stacked the books, nodding to herself, as she got to her feet. "One day, I'll leave this town," she whispered.

There was a booming sound from the hall.

I scrambled out from under the desk in time to see the library door fly open as a student fled inside. I could see the hallway behind him, the long wall of lockers next to the cafeteria. As I watched, red slashed across the lockers, and dripped down the wall.

Blood.

In the flash before the library door closed all the way, I saw students on the ground, and a figure above them: a girl, a girl with blond hair.

"Where's my locker?" the ghost girl screamed.

"I hate this school," the sensitive one said.

That night, I didn't even try to sleep. I was dressed and at the window, waiting, ready to go. Finally, near midnight, I saw a figure leave the house and sneak across the lawn in a spray of moonlight. But it wasn't Tom.

It was my grandmother.

I heard her car start in the driveway. I saw headlights brighten the side of the house. Then a shadow appeared under my window. She was returning to the house; she had forgotten something, and as she walked up the path, she looked up once, right at my window.

I gasped. I sprang back into the shadows, as if I had been shocked. It was instinct, of course, that made me move. She couldn't have really seen me.

I crept out of my room as quickly as I could. Downstairs, I heard sounds in the kitchen: my grandmother searching in drawers and cabinets for whatever she was looking for. The front doors of the house had been thrown wide open. I slipped through them, down the steps, and—though it was Tom I had been planning to follow—I snuck into the back-seat of my grandmother's idling car, curling up on the floor.

The driver's side door opened and my grandmother got in. She fastened her seat belt and drove. I listened to the rumble of the engine, feeling every bump in the road. I could see only a little: the backseat above me, where my grandmother had thrown her bag. A candle poked out and something else did too: a long thin stick, forked on the end.

My grandmother didn't drive far. Soon, we had stopped again. She opened the back door, then shut it. I heard her footsteps fading, and far off, a doorbell ringing on a house. Only then did I open my eyes. The big black bag was gone. I crawled out of the backseat and left the car.

The car was parked in a driveway before an ordinary two-story house, white with red shutters. The lawn looked neat and bare. There was another car parked in front of my grandmother's station wagon, a minivan. I approached the front door. I saw lights inside the house, the yellow glow spilling out onto the lawn, but noticed no one in the rooms.

I eased the front door open. The living room looked still and empty. I heard voices in another room, speaking together, reciting something in unison.

Saint Michael the Archangel,
defend us in battle;
be our protection against the wickedness and snares ...

I entered the house and followed the voices. In the kitchen, a circle of people stood in front of the fridge. Their eyes were closed, and they were holding hands: a man, a woman with a baby in a harness on her chest, and my grandmother. My grandmother's voice sounded the strongest, sure and loud, leading the couple in words I had never heard before.

... by the power of God,
thrust into hell Satan and all the evil spirits
who prowl about the world seeking the ruin of souls.

It was a prayer. But when it was done, I shuddered.

My grandmother opened her eyes. "I think the baby should go," she said, and the group dropped hands.

"No," the woman said. "It targets her. It comes for her."

"The baby will be fine," my grandmother said.

"No. I'm not leaving her in her crib so that... that thing can get her."

"No one is going to *get her*," my grandmother said. She looked at the man.

He shrugged. "This was Cindy's idea."

"Well, are you with us or not? Do you believe or not?" There was a pause.

"Frank," the woman said, an edge to her voice.

"Okay, okay, I'm in," he said. "I'm in, okay? I believe."

My grandmother nodded. Her big black bag sat open on the kitchen table, and she went to it, taking out a white candle and lighting it with a match.

I stood in the doorway, confused. Was this why my grandmother had left in the middle of the night? What did I really know about my grandmother? I had been surprised to hear her voice leading the chant in the kitchen, so strong and clear. I was surprised, and a little proud, by how she ordered the couple around. She was in charge. She knew what she was doing.

Whatever that was.

She took something out of the bag.

"Are you going to take pictures?" the man—Frank—said.

"No," my grandmother said.

"Because I saw on television, these guys on a show—they took pictures. And things showed up in the pictures."

"Things?"

"Orb things. You know."

"No," my grandmother said. "I'm sure I don't know."
It was a tape recorder she had pulled from her bag, an
old handheld one with a cassette tape. She pressed the red
record button.

"What are you doing?" Frank said.

"Shh," my grandmother said. "Listen." She held the tape
recorder out and slowly paced the kitchen, holding the device
before her as she circled the stove and sink, running it under
the cabinets.

It was like she was listening to the appliances. I would
have felt uncomfortable, embarrassed at the ridiculousness
of what she was doing, except my grandmother was so
commanding, I couldn't look away from her. Neither could
Frank and Cindy. Even the baby watched.

A new voice whispered, "I never know what to say."

A woman stood in the living room behind me.

I flattened myself against the doorway in case the woman
was going to enter the kitchen, in case she was going to try
and get by me—or through me. I had to remember: even
invisible, I took up space.

But the woman didn't move. "Do you?" she asked. "Do
you have any memorable words?"

I waited. My grandmother didn't seem to have heard the
woman, instead continuing to circle the kitchen as the couple
watched. I glanced back at the woman.

She was looking right at me.

"Me?" I whispered. "Me?"

She made a face. "Well, that's not very memorable."

She was speaking to me. She had seen *me*. I flinched so hard
I hit the pot rack, skillets and saucepans crashing to the floor.

Frank shouted, and Cindy clutched her baby. "I told you,"
Cindy said. "I told you."

"Impressive," the new woman said.

I stared at her. She had messy hair and wild eyes. "Who are you?" I said.

"Kate," the woman said, crossing her arms. "And I was here first."

"What do you mean? Can you see me?"

"I mean, *shove off*," Kate said. She uncrossed her arms and pushed me.

I failed and hit the wall, the last pot slamming to the ground.

My grandmother's eyes were searching the air. "Who's there?" she asked.

"Can you hear us?" Cindy shouted.

"Idiot," Kate said.

I turned at the sound of Kate's voice, confused. She had somehow moved to the other side of the kitchen, and stood on the stairs now. She looked at me pointedly, making sure I had seen her, then stomped up the steps.

My grandmother had turned too. "What's upstairs?" she asked.

"Nursery," Frank said.

"Oh no," Cindy said.

"Stay here," my grandmother said, but they didn't listen.

My grandmother reached the nursery first, and I was not far behind. Kate was already there, standing by the crib. "That woman," she said. "That woman is a terrible mother."

"Her?" I said, pointing to Cindy, who was crying softly and jiggling the baby in the harness. "She seems a little high strung, but I'm sure she's all right."

"All right?" Kate said. "All right?"

There was a mobile above the crib, dangling and bobbing as a tinkling sound played. Kate swept out her arm and tore it from the ceiling, flinging it across the room. The mobile hit the wall and broke into a dozen tinkling pieces. Cindy screamed, but my grandmother stayed calm, holding out the forked stick from her bag.

"It's all right to leave the baby alone," Kate mocked. "Even for a minute. It's all right to put the baby's favorite blanket over the lamp, to dim the lights when she's sleeping."

I looked at the lamp on a table by the crib. Cindy had in fact done just that, covered the lampshade with a baby blanket, pink and ratty on the ends.

"Well, that seems like a fire hazard," I said. "But the light's off now, so I'm sure it's fine. Who are you, anyway? The babysitter?"

"Idiot!" Kate said again. She had moved up to Cindy, and was shouting it in her face. Cindy wouldn't stop sobbing. The baby began to cry.

My grandmother addressed the air, holding the stick out. The long branch made a handle, the ends forming a *y*. "Spirit," my grandmother said. "Can you tell us your name?"

Kate shoved the changing table.

"How did you die?" my grandmother said.

Kate tore a blanket in two.

"How did you die?" I said.

The ends of the blanket fluttered to the ground. Kate opened the closet. I thought she was going to throw something, to destroy another baby thing, but she only looked at me, showing me the inside of the closet door. The wood there looked black and seared.

I smelled it then, smelled the smoke and ash, heard the crackling, smelled the hair burning. "Fire," I whispered. "You weren't the babysitter. You were the mother. Years ago, here in this house. A fire killed you. And your baby."

Kate looked at me. Our eyes met. She nodded once, satisfied, then stepped through the closet door, disappearing into the scorched wood.

The baby stopped crying. Cindy stopped sobbing, and my grandmother put down her stick. "It's finished," she said. She ushered Frank and Cindy into the hall. On her way out, she whipped the blanket from the light. "Don't leave that there again," she said. "It's a fire hazard."

I waited until they had gone downstairs, and I heard the sounds of plates and cups clattering and a kettle being filled. I heard my grandmother in the kitchen, talking about payment, and Frank trying to haggle. I sank onto my knees in the nursery. All around me lay Kate's destruction: wood splinters, string and wire from the mobile, cotton batting from the blankets.

But the room felt silent and empty. I was alone. The closet door had closed, and I knew without knowing why that my grandmother was right—that the spirit of Kate *was* gone. Gone for good. She had done what she needed to do, and moved on.

That was what ghosts needed, that was what kept them here after death. They had to get what they wanted. They had a task or a message or a job unfulfilled. It seemed so simple: to warn another mother, to ensure that no one else made Kate's own terrible mistake. That was what made Kate a ghost, an angry frustrated ghost. That was what kept her hanging around, haunting the room where she and her baby had died.

Was Tom trying to warn someone too? And if so, who? Why was he a ghost?

And what was my grandmother doing in the middle of the night, at what appeared to be the home of strangers, with sticks and candles and prayers?

That question I knew the answer to, even if I didn't want to believe it, even if I couldn't believe it. I knew. I think I had known all along. I think I had always suspected ... something: every time she paused, every time she listened, every time she cocked her head and looked off in the distance. It was not the distance she was seeing.

But watching her do it in person, witnessing what she was capable of, who she was—I shuddered. I made myself rise, pain beating in my back from the Stationmaster's burn and the bruising Kate had given me. Ghosts *could* hurt me, hurt me badly.

I slumped down the stairs, past the kitchen. They were sitting around the table now, talking, laughing, sipping tea. My grandmother bounced the baby on her lap. I made my way outside, into the car, and lay on the floor of the back-seat and cried.

My grandmother was a medium. My grandmother could see ghosts.

But my grandmother couldn't see me.

CHAPTER 9

What Do You Want?

I fell asleep in the car. When I woke up, sunlight streamed in through the windows, and someone was knocking on the glass. I sat up, my back and neck aching. Stiffly, I pulled myself up from the floor onto the backseat.

"It's unlocked," I said through the window.

Tom opened the door. I moved over to make room for him, and we sat side by side.

I thought of how many times I had sat next to Acid at school. We had sat this close. Closer. I had wanted Acid to kiss me, waited for it, though it never came. It seemed like another lifetime ago.

And I had thought I knew him, thought we might know each other better, thought he wanted to know me better too. But you didn't ever know anyone truly. You couldn't know anyone other than yourself, not really, not at all. People could leave. They could disappear without telling you. They could die.

They could die again.

What did I know about Tom, other than the fact that he

was dead? What did he like? We wouldn't have movies in common or TV. Had we read the same books? Did we have anything in common across a century?

"I read about you yesterday," I said. "I researched the orphan trains. Were you an orphan?"

"Not exactly," Tom said. "But it didn't make a lot of difference."

"Where did you come from?"

"New York. Like you." He brightened a bit. "It was better out here in the country. It seemed to be, anyway, at first. It was sunny and the air was sweet. I could breathe. There was space to run around, and they gave us good food on the train."

I wanted to ask him more about the train, about his life before and after, but he looked distant in the way I was learning meant he might drift in a moment; he might vanish in air. "I have to tell you something about my grandmother," I said. "She can see ghosts. That's where she went last night, to some house with some ghost. She makes a living from it, apparently."

"She can't see ghosts," Tom said. I started to protest, but then he said, "She can *hear* us, only hear us. And only sometimes, we think. Not all of us. She only hears Clara and Martha, we think. Only the girls." He shook his head. "I don't know. Sometimes I think she's listening to me too."

"Why didn't you tell me this?"

"It comes and goes. She's never tried to *talk* with us, not really. It just seems like she knows we're here. It feels like she's tolerating it. So, she doesn't bother us. We don't bother her." He paused. "Except for Clara."

I thought of Kate. I thought of the stick and the candle and the tape recorder and the strange chanting in the kitchen, the prayer. I remembered how my grandmother had known about the fire, known to take the blanket off the lamp.

"It's only sometimes that she seems to hear us, anyway. *Seems* to. And I don't think she makes much money for it, Ez, not enough to make a living. Not a lot of call for it. When she leaves at night, she only takes the black bag with the dowsing rod every now and then. Other times, she does go and nurse the sick." He paused again. "I've had many years to observe your grandmother."

I thought of the house: the candles cluttering the hallway, the dried herbs hanging from the rafters, the stray cats lounging around. If I looked at the spines of the books in the sitting room, would they all be about demons? Were there jars of rats' tails and eye of newt and snails in the cupboard?

"My grandmother hasn't helped you?" I asked. "All these years—she hears the dead—and she hasn't been able to help you?"

"I don't need help," Tom said. "Not from her—and not from you. You can get hurt by ghosts. I can't let it happen again."

"You should have thought of that before dying."

"I wish I had met you before dying."

This was the moment. I wanted him to kiss me. I willed him too. I knew if I stayed still, if I stayed quiet, if we didn't spook each other, he might. But I had to ask him something. "Tom," I said, "What do you want?"

He blinked at me. "What do you mean?"

I couldn't look away from his eyes, blue as a pond I dreamed, blue as a pond I had never actually seen. "I met a ghost last night. A woman. Her baby had died, and she just wanted to warn another mother whose baby was in danger. And once she did it—that was it. That was all she needed, to tell me that, to tell me and my grandmother so that we could save the baby. She got what she wanted, and then she went away. So tell me, Tom. What do you want?"

I had said too much—but it didn't matter. I grabbed his hand as if I could hold him still, as if I could keep him here in the car with me, keep him anywhere, make a ghost stay. "I need to know what you want," I said. "I need you to figure out why you're here, what's keeping you here, because you can't just disappear on me. The woman last night, the ghost? She got what she needed and then she was gone, in a heartbeat. She didn't say goodbye. She vanished. She went through a *door*. You can't do that to me."

"I won't, Ez," he said. "I promise."

But I didn't know if I believed him.

Martha didn't know what she wanted. "I have everything I need," she said, pulling a sheet from the wicker basket at her feet, the wind whipping the ends of the sheet around her legs. She hung the laundry on a rope strung between the barn and a tree.

My grandmother wasn't home, but I wondered what it would have looked like to her, what it looked like to someone on the road: the sheets sailing by all on their own, secured to the line by invisible hands.

"I have a nice home," Martha said. "A good position with a kind and decent family." She smiled at me.

The questions I wanted to ask her—*why did you die? What was missing from your life that's still missing?*—I couldn't bring myself to say. Those questions would dance around the other, central question of how she had done it and why.

I watched her shake another sheet from the basket, clothespin in her mouth, and hoist the sheet onto the line. "Can I at least help?" I asked.

She shook her head. "I've got my system."

"Martha, why did you decide to be a maid?"

At this, she laughed. "Decide? I didn't decide. I needed to work, needed to help out my family, to send money to them, so I did. I found a way. I did what I could. I'm good at it."

"Yes, you are," I said, watching the sheets catch the breeze and stiffen like a ship's sails. "And your family? Are any of them, you know, ghosts too?"

Did everyone become a ghost?

"Oh no, Miss," Martha said. She bent back to work. "They've all gone on. To a better place, I imagine."

I sat cross-legged, leaning back in the grass, and tried to imagine it: to have my family go on without me—and go where, exactly? Was that place any better than this one: this house, this work, this sunlight?

"This position was supposed to be temporary," Martha said. "Only until ..." She stopped. Her face went slack.

In the distance, I heard hammering. I waited. "Until what?" I said.

"Until I met a man and had a family," Martha whispered.

Hammering again. Sawing.

"Who's working on their house around here?" I asked.

The nearest neighbor was past the fairgrounds, and that house was a trailer. But Martha didn't answer me. She wasn't even looking at me. I followed her glance to the house, to its very top, where someone was standing on the roof.

My throat tightened. "What's he doing up there? What is that up there?"

"It's a widow's walk," Martha said. "For the wives of sailors at sea to watch for their husbands."

"Why is there a widow's walk in Pennsylvania?"

"Architectural folly," she whispered.

I rose, shielding my eyes against the sun. Backlit from a distance, the figure on the roof looked as thin and dark as a flame.

But Martha threw her arm out in front of me, stopping me from moving. She looked me right in the eyes. "Don't go up there," she said. "Don't you ever go up. It's not safe on the roof. Don't you ever."

"Okay," I said. By the time I looked back to the roof, the ghost was gone.

Mr. Black moaned, rolled his eyes, and ran his hands through his hair. "What do I want? What do I want? I want to be left alone. I want some peace and quiet. And whiskey!" He leaned back, his legs kicking, and not for the first time I worried he might topple from the gravestone where he was perched.

I shook my head. "I don't believe you. There's got to be something else, something you need, something keeping you here. Something big."

"That stinking mud hole of a pond," he said. "That's big. That kept me here."

"I thought you told me the pond was small, ornamental?"

"It's deep!" he said.

I fought a smile. Mr. Black was grumpy and drunk, but he had saved me from the Stationmaster. Twice. Maybe saved my life. I knew he was dependable. Martha had fetched him when the Stationmaster attacked me on the tracks, and he hadn't hesitated.

He watched her now, watched Martha below us, still hanging sheets by the barn. In the late afternoon, the wind was strong, and Martha's ghost work still wasn't done. Or maybe she was doing it again. Clouds raced across the sky, gray with blue undersides. When I looked at Mr. Black, he was smiling.

"Oh, watch the gusts now. They'll steal the sheet away. No, she's good. She's got it." He grinned at me. "Monday. Laundry day." His expression changed. "Why aren't you in school?"

"Um. Laundry day?"

He took a drink. "Fair enough."

We were sitting in the family cemetery above the house. It was a nice enough spot, when the wind blazed through, cooling my face, but I felt uneasy. Everywhere, all around us, gravestones poked out of the ground.

"Why do you hang out here all the time?" I asked.

"No reason," Mr. Black said. "I like the view."

In the valley below, the sheets fluttered in the wind. Martha wiped her hands on her dress.

"It's *Martha*!" I said. "Martha's the reason you're still here. You want Martha. You love her. You're a ghost because you never told Martha you love her!"

"I don't love her!" Mr. Black said. "My word! The living are crazy!" He looked horrified, then he looked down at his bottle, studying it as if it were fascinating or endlessly deep.

"Martha's never been kissed before," I said. "And I happen to know she wants to be."

He didn't look up. "Is that so?" A horn blasted in the distance, familiar to me now. "Keystone from New York City," Mr. Black said. "Right on schedule." His glance flickered up. "Oh no. You may want to avert your eyes, my dear."

"Why?"

"That's idiot's up on the roof again."

I looked up. The ghost stood on the widow's walk. "What's going on?" I said. "Who is he?"

In the yard, Martha stared up at the house, shielding her eyes, her laundry forgotten.

I rose. "What's happening?"

98

"I said don't look!" Mr. Black said. He leapt off the gravestone and clamped his hand over my eyes.

I swatted him. "You smell like an alley!" I said.

"You can't be trusted to close your own bloody eyes!"

"Why do I need to close my eyes?"

But Mr. Black wouldn't tell me, and he wouldn't move his hand.

And so I didn't see the Builder fall from the widow's walk of my grandmother's house, fall for the hundredth or more time and die. An accident, a terrible accident. Again. I heard Martha scream. Mr. Black dropped his hands, and I saw her running, holding her skirts. She streamed into the house. The laundry went slack on the line. One sheet tore loose and was trampled.

Xavier Vale started building his house in 1890. It took ten years—and he never really finished. He also never really let anyone else help. He fired workers, contractors, then did the work himself, scaring the neighbors, worrying the town. He kept adding rooms, even though he and his wife, Emily, only ended up having three children. He wanted more. He wanted to throw a big party when the house was finally done, to invite the whole town, to make peace with them, after all the hammering. The family *did* throw a party: it was a combination housewarming, New Year's Eve party—and a kind of wake. He died at the party, as did his maid.

And after the party, the gardener drowned.

Vale was the Builder, a ghost bent on reliving his death by returning to the roof, and Mr. Black was the gardener, but where did Martha fit in? Why had she died?

I closed the search window of the library computer, my eyes aching. It was hours before last period and the bus

99

to take me home. It was also the last day of school before summer break, and every few minutes, there was whooping in the hallway. On the bus ride in, I had witnessed two boys showing off cans of shaving cream stashed in their backpacks.

I was wondering if there was a spot in the back of the library where I could just curl up and read a book, away from the librarian, when the door breezed open. I heard a snatch of conversation from the hall, a question I recognized.

"Can you help me find my locker?"

This time I didn't wait for blood to appear on a wall. I didn't wait for a kid to be scared to the ground and bloodied, and for everyone to laugh and think he had tripped. I left the library.

The ghost girl stood there in the hallway, clutching her books, as I knew she would be. She saw me right away. It was startling to be seen.

"Can you help me?" she asked.

I tried to forget her strength, her anger. *Malicious*, Tom had called her.

"Yes," I said.

"I can't find my locker."

"Do you know the number?"

Wordlessly, she turned her hand over so that I could see her palm, where she had written the numbers in marker, childish green ink smearing her skin.

"696," I read. How long had it been written there? Years? Decades?

The girl put her hand down.

"Okay," I said. "The six hundred lockers are in the next hall, by the computer classrooms." From what I could see of the courtyard through the windows, a jumble of shaving cream and limbs, many students weren't in the classrooms. *Any* classrooms. "Let's go now, okay?"

"Really?" she said. "You're really going to help me? Far out." She was friendly, sweet even, sticking close to my shoulder as she followed. There was no sign in her of the rage that had made blood appear on a wall. "Are you a senior?" she asked.

"Sophomore," I said.

"Really? I dig your hair. Is that henna?"

I looked at her. "Um, no. It's just black."

"Cool," the girl said.

We had reached the right hallway, and I trailed my fingers across the lockers. Most had been decorated for the end of school with streamers and glittery signs. But 696, when we found it, was bare, banged up. There wasn't even a lock.

I tugged but the door didn't open. "That's funny," I said. I pulled at the handle again, but it was stuck, rusted shut. "I'm not sure this is gonna work."

The girl reached up, balled her hand into a fist, and pounded the locker hard. The door swung open.

"Wow," I said. "You're going to fit right in around here."

Now she would do it. Now she would disappear or fade away, or do whatever it was that Kate had done, whatever it was that ghosts did when their mission was accomplished, their want fulfilled, and they could go, just go. Go … wherever. I didn't want to think about where that was; I just wanted the girl to go there.

But she didn't.

She peeked into the locker. She was so short, she had to creep up on tiptoe to do it. The locker was empty.

"There's nothing there," I said, my stomach tightening. What was she looking for? What if she got angry again? What did she *want*?

"One thing's there," the girl said. She tore away a piece of paper that had been taped to the inside of the door, and handed it to me. "Take a look."

It was a newspaper clipping, yellowed and creased. The headline read: **SEARCH FOR MISSING GIRL ENDS IN TRAGEDY**. There was a picture.

I turned to the girl. She was gone. I scanned the hallway. It was deserted. I heard a squealing, and turned to see the boys from my bus, sliding across the linoleum floor at the end of the hall, covered in shaving cream. I looked at the girl in the picture again. Her hair looked neat and combed, parted in the middle. She wore wide-legged jeans and a shirt with daisies. There were no circles under her eyes, and she was smiling. She didn't look tired or angry or malicious at all.

Not yet.

June 5, 1976, the paper read. **A missing Wellstone High freshman has been found dead.**

CHAPTER 10

Can You See Me?

Clara sat on the library cart and watched me on the computer. As I grew more and more frustrated, she grew more and more bored. There wasn't much information on Louise Parker, the girl from the article, the ghost from the hall: only a few sites noting her death, and many more speculating that she was haunting the high school (apparently she had been looking for her locker for quite some time).

At first, I thought the lack of information was due to the age of Louise's case. Her death was more than thirty years old, and even news of a murder or suicide—no one seemed sure—fades after awhile. But then I realized the true reason Louise Parker didn't have many sites devoted to her.

There were too many *other* dead or missing.

Almost every year someone went missing in Wellstone, or in the small towns around Wellstone, a grisly tradition stretching back as far as I could find. The names crowded over each other: *Sandra, Victoria, Sarah, Ted...* They sounded so ordinary, so normal. But they had vanished.

"They're not all ghosts so don't go looking for them," Clara said. She was stretched out on top of the book cart, reclining over a stack of encyclopedias.

"How do you know?" I asked.

"Tom and I would have met them by now."

"But you're saying they're all dead? All of these missing kids are dead?"

She shrugged. "Maybe."

Sandra, Victoria, Sarah, Ted...

"What happened to them?" I asked.

"Different things. Drowning and hanging and being hit by automobiles. And being hit by trains. And, what are they called? Drugs."

"Oh," I said.

"And running away. A lot of running away."

Wellstone was small, suffocating—it was true. There was no mall. There wasn't even a movie theater. New York was a day's drive, but who had the money to go there? Who had any money at all? The houses were collapsing, taken back by the bank, or surrendered, sold to no one. Many of the houses weren't houses but trailers. The lawns were overgrown, the businesses abandoned.

I hadn't actually had a conversation with anyone living in Wellstone, not anyone alive, but what would they have thought of me, if they could have seen me: the Chinese-American orphan girl from the city, sent here as punishment for trespassing? Would I ever make a friend here? Everyone already thought my grandmother was a witch.

And they were kind of right.

I turned back to the computer.

"Why are you such a bore?" Clara said. "Tom and I thought you'd be levitating things by now. Throwing candles and moving chairs and writing messages on foggy windows. There are lots of fun things you can do, you know, and you never even do them."

"Like what?" I said glumly.

"You could steal candy. And you could actually eat it. And ribbons. And wear them. So many things you could do, Esmé! We don't know why you don't do them."

"We?" I said.

"Me and Tom."

I saw her reflection in the computer screen, her hazy shape leaning forward. I heard her whisper icily in my ear. But I didn't feel her breath; she had no breath. "He doesn't love you, you know."

I jerked away, pushing the chair out from the desk and standing. I didn't care if the librarian or anyone saw. I stared at Clara.

"I know Tom kissed you," she said. "Martha's seething with jealousy. Everyone's talking. But I'm the only one who knows why he did it."

"*Why?*" I echoed.

I felt a strange tightness in my chest and limbs, a buzzing in my ears. I didn't know what to feel first, anger over Clara or fear about Martha being jealous. Martha who laughed with me, who helped me decide what to wear, who sat on the end of my bed and tucked me in. Martha who was like my sister now that my sister wasn't here.

Clara drew her knees together, clicking her heels against the cart. "Tom thinks he'll move on if he loves you. He thinks he'll stop being a ghost. You know if you get what you want on earth you can go away? You can stop haunting this place, this backwoods town, stop reliving your death every stupid boring day."

"I know," I said, weakly. "I'm the one who figured that out."

"Well, we always suspected that was it, you know. You're just so direct, Esmé." She flipped her hair. "Tom was never kissed in life. So when you came along, he hatched the plan at once."

"The plan?"

"To make you love him. To make you kiss him. He hasn't gone away yet, so he thinks he has to do more. He wants to go further."

I felt my legs go wobbly and I leaned against the chair. The burn on my back, which had been healing, felt fresh as the day it had happened. My head pounded, and seemed to be full of sound. I couldn't stop thinking of Tom. I thought of him in my grandmother's car. I thought of him at the pond. And I thought of him in the cafeteria, how his lips had been like anyone's lips, except I wanted him to kiss me.

I remembered everything I thought I knew about love, which was nothing. Acid never called. He never emailed, or texted, or wrote. He would never visit me here, I knew. He wanted to be around me only when I was close, when I was convenient. I thought Tom was different than other guys, but what did I know?

He was dead. That was the only difference.

My eyes clouded over and I couldn't see Clara anymore. All the encyclopedias on the cart had spilled out onto the floor. What did I know of Tom, really? He was half an orphan, he had come from the city, he had stolen things. But what were his dreams before dying? What had he hoped to be? Was he capable of hurting me? Who *was* he? I thought of him running in the moonlight. I thought of him lying still on the tracks. I thought of him crying. I started to cry.

"It's okay," the library aide, the sensitive one, said to no one, to the air—hearing me, but not seeing me. No one saw me. "It's okay."

I waited in line for the bus alongside boys covered in shaving cream.

They were laughing. Everyone was laughing. One boy, the one who had called my grandmother a witch, jiggled water balloons in his arms. The buses were late. I heard the students talking; someone had egged windows down in the garage. There were cheers, once the news spread, which I didn't understand. Late buses meant everyone would be getting home late, late on the last day of school.

"Guess some things don't change."

I didn't have to turn to know who said it. I tightened my hold on my bag. I made myself say nothing.

"In my time, we had tin cans and firecrackers and frogs. You don't want to know what that combination makes."

I still didn't answer. I didn't turn.

"The bus will take forever," Tom said. A bit of pleading had come into his voice. "Why don't you skip it, Ez, and we can walk home together? Clara said you found out about the runaways. I've met some, you know, over the years, some that were dead, some that were ghosts like us for a time. No one's lasted as long as we have, but Clara says—"

I spun around, so fast that the boy next to me fumbled and dropped one of his water balloons. It broke with a splat. "Clara says your plan isn't working," I said.

"One of these nights it will," he said quietly.

"One of these nights when you'll—what? Sleep with me?"

I saw something flicker over Tom's face. "Stop it, Ez. I don't like this."

"Right. And I know now why you like me. Well, I'm sorry it didn't work out the first time. I'm sorry you didn't move on or disappear or go into the light or whatever when you kissed me, because you're not getting a second chance. You're not getting close to me again. I won't let anyone close to me ever again."

"What are you talking about, Ez?" Tom said, moving forward.

"Get back," I said, and I pushed him.

Ghosts could hurt me. Ghosts could wound me, shove me, draw blood from me, knock me down, bruise me, burn me. Because I was invisible. Because I was lost. Because I was nothing.

But I could hurt ghosts too.

Tom fell when I pushed him, knocking into the boy with the water balloons. The boy turned, thinking someone was messing with him, and lobbed a balloon at no one, at the air. But the balloon struck me.

I didn't flinch. The balloon broke against my folded arms. The cold water felt like a punch in the stomach. But I still didn't move.

"Whoa," the boy said. He and his friends backed up.

"It broke before it hit the ground!" one of them said.

"Cheap plastic," the first boy said as the buses careened into the lot.

Students started to move, to hug goodbye, get their yearbooks signed. I stayed rooted with my arms folded, dripping and cold. I watched Tom pick himself off the ground and back away from me.

"All right, Ez," he said. "I didn't want you to get hurt. I didn't want you to get involved in my death. I've done too much already."

"Yeah," I said. "You have."

"I won't bother you again," he said. And he faded into the crowd, replaced by students, real live students with books and balloons, surging forward onto the buses. They pushed past me. I let them bump into me. One dropped a book from his open bag and just left it, got on the bus without looking back.

I picked up the book. It had a green cover with an embossed gold frame. The yearbook. He had left his yearbook, full of people I wouldn't know. I flipped to the first page anyway: a dedication, a full-page photograph of a boy, skinny, with glasses and red hair. *In Memoriam*, the script at the bottom read.

I turned to Tom, but he was gone.

When I checked my phone on the bus, there were several messages from the Firecracker. The bus dropped me off, and I called her back without listening to them first.

"What have you done to Grandma?" she said.

"Hi to you too," I said.

"Esmé, she is so upset."

"Upset?"

"She called me twice last night. Twice. First, Grandma never calls. Second, she was crying. Crying. What's happening? What did you do?"

"I didn't do anything." Then I remembered the food I had slowly been swiping from the pantry and fridge, the dishes I had washed and tried to replace in the right spots, the showers I took when I thought she wasn't home. "What did she tell you?"

"That's the thing. She won't say. She won't give me specifics. She only says you're in trouble."

Trouble?

"It's your fault for sending me here," I said. "This place is bad luck for people my age. Some kid disappears like, every year. Some of them don't make it home. Every year—did you know that? This town is cursed. And you thought it was going to be good for me?"

"This isn't my fault," the Firecracker said. "We're talking about you here. *She's in trouble. She's in trouble.* That's all Grandma says. Esmé, what trouble? What is going on over there?"

I had made it to the top of the driveway. I stopped. My grandmother's car was parked by the barn. She was home.

"Gotta go," I said into the phone and hung up.

I turned the corner of the house to find Martha on the front steps. A basket sat beside her, and half a dozen of the cats zigzagged over her lap, crawling in and out of the basket. I remembered what Clara had said, about her being jealous.

I wished I had never gotten off the bus.

"Hello there," Martha said. She was sewing something, looking down at her work, not at me. Maybe she couldn't bear to look at me. "How was school?"

"Fine," I said.

"Last day, was it? How did it go?"

"Fine."

"Did anyone see you?"

"No."

She set her work down. "Miss, what's wrong?"

"Nothing," I said. My bag felt heavy, pressing on my burn.

Martha returned to her sewing. "Well, your grandmother's home early, and she's not happy. I'm concerned about her. I think you should look in on her."

"Look in on her? How am I supposed to look in on her? She can't see me. She can't hear me."

"Miss?"

I exploded. "It's not my fault that Tom went after me. It's not my fault he kissed me. I didn't know!"

"Didn't know?"

"What he was doing. What he was planning. And that you'd be mad."

"Mad?" Martha stared at me. "I'm not mad. I'm happy for you, and for Tom. I've been hoping for decades he would find a young miss. Of course, I had hoped she would be *dead*. But no one is perfect."

She patted a spot on the step beside her. I dropped my bag and sat, scooping up a cat to make room. The Manx hissed and swiped at me. "Can the cats see you?" I asked.

"Yes. More bothersome than anything really." Martha fished a cat out of her basket and set it on the ground.

"Are they grandmother's—what are they called—*familiars*?"

"No," Martha laughed. "They're strays. They live in the barn. Your grandmother feeds them and we pet them. They like the attention. They get more of it from ghosts than from the living, I suspect. Now," she turned to me, "what do you mean, *planning*? I don't think Tom planned for you. I don't think he planned to feel the way he might feel about you."

I fell silent. Sitting on the steps, in the sunlight with Martha, it was easy to question Clara. Was she lying? I had listened to her.

I watched Martha's hands. "What are you working on?"

"Darning your socks. I can't work like I used to. But I have to do something."

"Is it boring, being a ghost?"

"Yes," she said. "It is. A person would like to stop it, if they could."

111

She didn't seem jealous. She seemed sad. I wanted to talk with her about Tom, to ask her if she knew why he had kissed me, why he liked me—he barely even knew me—if he did. But I stayed quiet, petting a cat who had wandered close. I asked Martha. "How did you die?"

For a long time, she was silent. Finally she said: "In the kitchen. I died in the kitchen. So I don't go there anymore. I don't cook. I can't help you with your meals or cleaning up. I can't go in there. I'm sorry about that."

"It's okay," I said.

She folded the last socks in neat pairs and stood, balancing the basket on her hip, the work done, the conversation over. "Your grandmother's home early and she's in a way. You should look in on her."

"Okay," I said. I rose. "Thanks for talking with me."

"Congratulations on your last day of school, Miss. If I could go in the kitchen, I'd bake you a cake. I was good at baking, I think."

I found my grandmother in the sitting room. It was the only place I ever saw her, really, sitting on the stiff flowered couch with the crocheted back, watching television—often with the sound off. Usually she was gone when I came home from school, at the store or running errands, and she often worked through the night. This was strange, Martha said, her being here in the afternoon, and I knew it. And I knew to go to the sitting room once I entered the house because of the voice.

Someone was talking. It filled the hall, a female voice, high and young. I looked behind me for Martha, but she was gone; only the basket sat by the open door. Already the socks were unfolding themselves, holes opening up at the toes. Martha's work, the work of the dead, was undoing itself.

I followed the voice.

By the time I reached the stairs, I had recognized it as mine.

It made me walk faster. What was my grandmother listening to? How could she have a recording of me? Was it an old video? I turned into the sitting room. The television was off, and my grandmother lay on her back on the sofa. She didn't move when I entered the room. She didn't see me, or hear me. I was surprised by the disappointment I felt at this—from my grandmother, the medium.

I wasn't a ghost, I reminded myself. I wasn't dead. Why would she sense me?

My grandmother had closed her eyes. A cloth lay across them. She was lying in the dark room, listening to a tape recorder she held close to her ear. It was the small, portable recorder she had taken to Kate's house. Without removing the cloth from her eyes, or hardly moving at all, my grandmother stopped the tape, rewound it, and played it again.

I heard my own voice, threading through the machine. "*Me? Me?*" I said on the tape. "*Where are you? What do you mean? Can you see me?*"

My grandmother made a sound. She stopped the tape, rewound it.

"*Me? Me?*"

I crept into the room. I stood over my grandmother, listening as she listened. There were long pauses in between my words, as if someone else was answering me.

Someone was.

It was the conversation in the kitchen, the conversation I had with Kate. The tape recorder had worked. It had picked something up—but not a ghost sound, as my grandmother had probably hoped, not the sound of the woman haunting the couple's nursery. The tape recorder had picked up her own granddaughter's voice.

I was the ghost on my grandmother's tape.

"*Where are you? What do you mean? Can you see me?*"

"Grandma," I broke into my own voice. "Grandma," I talked over myself, trying to reach her. I shook the back of the couch. But she never looked up. She never heard me, the real me.

I stood by her side as she rewound the tape, listening again and again.

CHAPTER 11

Mixed Up

My grandmother thought I was dead.

This was complicated by the fact that my grandmother *saw* the dead—heard them, at least; could sense them sometimes, according to Tom—and yet she couldn't find me, her own granddaughter.

I had spent my time in Wellstone going out of my way to avoid being detected by her, being quiet, covering my tracks, not wanting to confuse or scare her. Now I needed her to see me, to know me, to know I was all right. I was fine. Just … invisible. I spilled flour on the counter in the kitchen and wrote: *I'M ALIVE*. When the bathroom mirror fogged after a shower, I wrote a note on the glass. I didn't clean up after myself. I convinced Martha to stop making my bed (it unmade itself in a few hours, anyway).

"She still thinks you're dead," Clara said. "She just thinks you don't know it yet. Which is the worst kind of being dead. Also, she thinks you're a slob."

"Were you ever like that?" I asked.

"A slob?"

"No. Did you ever not know you were dead?"

We were out on the driveway. I didn't want to speak to Clara, not after what she had said to me in the library, but I would walk away from her and she would only appear in the next place. She haunted me. I couldn't shake her.

"No," Clara said. "I knew I was dead. I welcomed it."

I bent down for a stone, not looking at her. "Did you ... were you like Martha? Did you do it to yourself?"

But Clara didn't seem offended. She didn't seem like anything at all. She knew what I meant and shrugged. "No," she said. "It wasn't that. My death was an accident. I had a plan to do something. But the plan didn't work." She was walking back and forth on one of the railroad ties that divided the yard from the driveway, balancing on the rotting beam as if in a circus, her arms outstretched. "I was cold. It was winter. Our shack wasn't heated. And I thought a fire might do ... *other* useful things."

"A fire?"

"Yes." She dropped her arms and looked at me. "I burned to death. Are you impressed?"

"No. That sounds awful." I studied her face for emotion. She looked blank, consciously blank. She had hardened herself. She had switched off. "Clara, I'm so sorry."

"I didn't plan on burning myself up. But it was a better death than if *he* had done it."

"He?" I asked.

"The Stationmaster. My father." Clara smiled when she said the word; I remembered Tom had spit it out. She hopped off the railroad tie, and kicked the pebbles I had lined up on the asphalt, slowly spelling out *H-I*, my message to my grandmother. Clara swept them neatly down the drive. We watched them roll into the road.

116

Supervision

"Great," I said. "Thanks a lot." I looked at Clara, her white-blond hair, perfectly waved, frozen in that style for a century. She was often scowling or humming or talking to herself. *Disturbed*, Martha called her. *Damaged. Not her fault*, Martha said. Tom said Clara meant well, was doing the best she could. "What did the Stationmaster do to you?" I asked. "Why did he adopt either of you? Why was he ever allowed?"

"Because we were left," Clara snapped. "Because we were both the last ones at the station, and it was his station, and if he didn't take us home with him, they were going to send us back to New York."

I thought of the apartment in New York: small and cluttered, noisy and expensive. "The city's all right."

"I would have been sent back to my mother," Clara said. "My mother was a working mother, and she said I was almost the right age." A scattering of pebbles was still left on the driveway. Clara picked them up and began to throw them, one by one, at the road.

"Why did the Stationmaster want to adopt kids?"

"I don't know." Clara hit the mailbox with a rock. "He wanted company." She hit a tree. "He wanted control. He wanted someone to keep house for him, and cook for him, and work the garden." Some of the cats had wandered over from the house and were sniffing at her. Clara stroked one with her free hand. "And sometimes?" Clara said, her hand tightening around the cat's neck. "Sometimes, you just need something to kick." The cat loped away from her, yowling. "It was all right when Tom was around. There were two of us. We stuck together, looked out for each other. We kept each other safe. But after Tom died? There was no one to keep me safe. So I died. Only to have the Stationmaster follow me."

117

"Clara," I said. "What do you want?"

Clara wasn't like Tom. She wasn't like Mr. Black, with whom I'd had to guess, or Martha who confessed in whispers, or the Builder, Xavier Vale, the ghost I still didn't know anything about. Clara just told me.

"For my brother to be happy," she said.

I walked back alone to the house, trudging through the grass. With every shove through the weeds—why didn't my grandmother ever mow?—I tried to forget Tom, how his name sent a shiver down my spine. I tried to concentrate on another mystery. Back in my room, I took the folded clipping from my backpack and read it again.

Louise was fourteen. She had never come home from her afterschool job, babysitting just a few streets away from her own house. She was last seen just before twilight. The father of the family she babysat for had offered her a ride home, but she decided to walk.

It wasn't even dark, after all.

Her body was found by the railroad tracks. There were no suspects.

I thought of the picture in the paper, the girl's faraway smile. I wished I could talk to my grandmother, to ask her questions, if she knew so much about ghosts. The ghost Louise hadn't disappeared until after she had shown me the article taped to her locker. Was that all she wanted, for someone to know? Or did she want me to solve her murder? How was I supposed to solve a murder? Was this the kind of thing my grandmother did?

I couldn't sleep that night, and when the train whistle blew at midnight, I was ready, headed out the front door and onto the lawn before the first blast even faded. In my pocket, I had a small black vial my sister had given me back in New York.

I don't know what I expected to see. Maybe Tom. Maybe my grandmother getting into the car with her big bag of tricks. But what I found at the station, what I saw on the tracks in front of the stopped, heaving train, as I leaned over the platform, wasn't Tom. Or the Stationmaster.

It was another body.

"Ez, get out of here." Tom stepped out of the shadows of the roof overhang, holding a wrench.

"You can't tell me what to do," I said. "You're staying out my life, remember?"

He clutched the wrench. "This is my fight, my death. It doesn't concern you."

I looked down at the tracks, at the ghost lying still. I couldn't turn away. The face of the ghost was turned down. I could see a skinny form, long legs in jeans, long pale arms in a T-shirt—the arms just tossed over the tracks, tangled and contorted in a way no living body would be, in a way that made me sick. "Tom, who is that?"

"You need to leave."

I blinked back the tears that burned my eyes. Queasiness rose up in my stomach, but I looked harder at the tracks. "He's wearing sneakers." And the lettering on the back of his T-shirt read ... Wellstone High.

I leaned over the edge. "Tom, I know that kid. I've seen him before. His picture was in the yearbook. *This* year's yearbook. It was dedicated to him. That boy died just this year."

Tom took my arm. "You need to get out of here now." But then he went limp. He lost the wrench, dropping it onto the platform with a resounding clang. It was as if all the energy went out of him, as if someone had cut a string and released him.

119

Something was moving toward us, a light that bobbed. A lantern.

The Stationmaster was coming.

"Tom," I whispered, but his eyes were frozen on the lantern in the distance. I couldn't watch him die again. I grabbed Tom's shirt and pulled him back into the shadows of the stationhouse overhang. We were close, closer than we'd ever been, closer even than when he'd kissed me.

"Shut up," I said to him, although he was not talking.

The Stationmaster came into view. He strode to the front of the train and bent down before it, studying the boy. The redheaded boy. The dead boy.

Then with a jerking sound, a sickening, almost mechanical cracking of bones straightening into place, and muscles remembering their form, the boy stood. The dead boy made a sound, not a breath—a long rattling sigh. He was taller than the Stationmaster, but skinny, so skinny. He looked very surprised.

"What's going on?" I whispered to Tom.

"I don't know," he said.

The Stationmaster didn't seem shocked to see the boy stand, and he didn't take long to react. He reared his arm back and swung, bringing the lantern down with a crack. I flinched.

The lantern didn't hit the boy, but it scared him. He cried out and fell. Then he got back up again.

"I don't understand," I said. "That boy *died*. The yearbook said."

"He's a ghost," Tom said. "He's reliving his death."

"*Your* death. That's your death out there. He's reliving what happened to you, isn't he, how you died? Unless ..." I faltered, watching the boy rise and fall, rise and fall. "Unless ..."

The Stationmaster turned. He searched the shadows where we stood, the whites of his eyes flashing almost yellow. "Tom Griffin? Is that you, boy?"

"Ez, go."

Before I could protest, Tom had jumped onto the tracks. Now there were two boys, circling the Stationmaster, but it didn't seem to slow him down at all. He swung the lantern as if it were a club, first at one boy, then at the other. The lantern sizzled as it struck. Tom was hit on the shoulder and flung backward.

I gasped, and the Stationmaster turned. "Who else is there?"

I waited, holding my breath, in the dark.

"Clara, honey, is that you?"

"Leave her alone!" Tom said.

The Stationmaster reared back to hit him. He would kill him. He would kill Tom just as he did every night. And then he would come for me. And kill me too.

The old man's back was turned, raising the lantern. The other boy was down. I saw my chance, and I dashed from the shadows, my finger posed on the red trigger of the small black vial, the bottle from my sister. It didn't hurt, and I knew it wouldn't last: it hadn't happened to him in life. I was pretty sure they didn't even have it in his lifetime.

But the pepper spray surprised the Stationmaster. He set down his lantern to wipe at his eyes, giving me enough time to run. I ran for the hill. I ran for the house. I ran without looking back, knowing behind me Tom was going to die again.

"That's ridiculous," Mr. Black said.

"I know it," I said. "I know it's true. The Stationmaster killed Tom, and he killed that redheaded boy. And I wouldn't be surprised if he killed Louise, too."

"Who's Louisa again?"

121

"Louise. I told you. A girl from school. Another ghost."

"Well, I'm glad you figured all that out." Mr. Black was sitting on the porch railing on the second story of my grandmother's house—a little close to the edge for my comfort, but as he pointed out, what was he going to do, die? He had a licorice root he had found somewhere clamped in his mouth, further garbling his already mumbled speech. I knew he couldn't taste it. "Nice story," Mr. Black said. "Very imaginative. Extra points for creativity. But the dead can't kill the living. Believe me. I've tried."

"What does that mean?"

"Never mind. The most a ghost could do to anyone—except apparently you—is scare them."

"So the Stationmaster scared that boy to death. He gave him a heart attack, or he caused him to fall and hit his head. He lured the boy to his death. I know he did the same to Louise."

Mr. Black looked away from me, toward the road. "Wait a moment," he said. "Just wait."

I hugged my knees to my chest. I changed the subject. "Can I ask you something? Do you think Tom is a good person? Trustworthy?"

Mr. Black gave a shrug. "He's dead. Trustworthy enough."

"Clara told me something about him."

"Ha," Mr. Black said. "Well, there's your issue. No good comes from that girl. She told Martha lies about me, you know. Poisoned her against me."

"Really? What did she say?"

"Said I was a drunk."

"You are a drunk."

"Well," Mr. Black chewed on the licorice. "She didn't have to tell her."

I looked at the floor of the balcony, at the empty bottles, dusty blue and black, that were collecting there.

"Why did you drink that night, the night you died? What happened?"

"It wasn't drinking that killed me," Mr. Black said. "It was drinking and *swimming*." He bit the licorice in half, looked down at the pieces, then threw the stick over the railing. "It was a bad time. The Builder had a terrible accident—everyone saw—and then Martha …"

"What happened to Martha?"

He shook his head. "She was sad, very sad. She made a mistake. She got her feelings mixed up." He pointed his finger at me. "Don't you go getting your feelings mixed up. Don't you go falling for the wrong lad, one that doesn't deserve you."

"What do you mean? Do you mean Tom?"

But Mr. Black had seen something on the road. He slid off the railing and stood. "Battle stations," he said.

I scrambled to my feet. "What are we doing here again?"

"Once a month," Mr. Black reached into the pocket of his black jacket, and pulled out a fistful of pebbles, which he passed over to me, "the town sends a dogcatcher out."

"Dogcatcher?"

"Technically, a catcatcher. He tries to round up the Manxes, and take them to the pound. Certain death. Cats being killed! We can't have that, can we?"

"Because the cats can see you? See ghosts?" I asked. I held the pebbles with both hands, as Mr. Black reached into his coat and pulled out more. I didn't stop to wonder why he had rocks in his pockets. Some slipped through my fingers, tumbling onto the balcony and rolling through the railing slats.

"No," Mr. Black said. "Because they're adorable. Here he comes." He fell silent, and I heard it: the car on the hill. "He barely makes it up the driveway. Bloody fool. Once or twice a year in the winter, he gets stuck."

The motor cut out. Soon I heard someone walking.

"Get ready," Mr. Black said. He motioned to me, and I came to stand behind him at the railing. I looked down but didn't see anything, only the yard, the cracked path leading to the house. Then I heard whistling. My stomach clenched. Whistling.

What was the matter with me? It was only the stupid dogcatcher.

Catcatcher.

"Wait till you see the shiny moon of his bald head," Mr. Black whispered.

"Here, kitty, kitty," I heard a voice say.

"Now!" Mr. Black said. He let loose his pebbles, flinging them over the rail. More and more seemed to appear from his pockets, an endless stream. He kept reaching in and dredging up more.

The man looked up, right where we stood, and I felt panic, panic at being caught—an old familiar feeling. I was caught in the subway tunnel. I was caught at school when I hadn't done my homework or had skipped class or just wasn't good enough. I was never good enough. Acid and I would sneak out to the boiler room, or the bodega down the street. He was never caught.

But I was. I was always in trouble. I was always seen.

This man couldn't see me, not now, not anymore—I knew this; I was starting to truly believe it. He saw the moldy roof, the crumbling railing of the balcony, the overgrown oaks and birches, and nothing more. He couldn't see me. Maybe this was all I got: invisibility.

And maybe I could do what I wanted.

I flung the stones over the rail. I threw them hard. Rocks rained down on the man, and he held up his arms to shield himself.

"Pick on someone your own size!" Mr. Black said.

124

The dogcatcher put his net over his head, trying to protect himself, the pebbles bouncing off his bald spot. He staggered back to his van, muttering, "That house should be condemned!"

"Great," I said, watching the man pull the door shut and start the engine. "Now he'll have the police out."

"No," Mr. Black said. "Too afraid. And no one would believe him. He comes every month and every month is the same. We chase him off. He comes back. Gives us a bit of fun. That's all we need, fun. Someone to react."

I thought of Clara dropping encyclopedias in the library, of Louise conjuring blood. Ghosts wanted people to notice them, to listen. I watched the van backed up and nearly hit the barn.

"The redheaded boy," I said. "He's not a ghost anymore. He's not hanging around here. And I think I know why. He got what he wanted. If you get what you want, if you do what you're meant to do, the last task you have left or whatever, you can go. Go ... wherever you go after death. You can move on. You don't have to be a ghost anymore. And the redheaded boy did it. He wanted me to see his death. He wanted me to know—for someone to know—the Stationmaster was responsible. And he wanted me to stop it from happening to anyone else."

Mr. Black said nothing. He tipped the last pebble out of his pocket and flung it over the rail. It landed with a soft pinging sound on the driveway.

"Where did you get so many rocks?" I asked. "How did they fit in your pockets?"

He shrugged. "Old habit. I used them once before. Rocks make very good weights."

CHAPTER 12

Door to Nowhere

The books on ghosts and hauntings were hard to find. They were all hidden: squashed in the corners, shelved behind other books, slipped behind the bookcases, and sheeted in dust. It was as if my grandmother didn't want anyone to know she had those books, that she read those kinds of things, even though she had lived alone for over a decade.

She was still keeping who she was a secret.

I fished a book out from behind the piano, a heavy one. I was brushing the dust off, and noticing the cobweb shawl dangling from my arm when Tom appeared.

"Ez, you're wasting your time," he said. "Mr. Black told me your idea, and it doesn't make any sense. A ghost killing the living? Luring them to their deaths?"

I looked at him. "I'm standing in my grandmother's sitting room, my grandmother who's a medium; I'm invisible—and I'm talking to a ghost. What about that doesn't make sense?" I shook off the cobweb. "Have you seen the redheaded ghost since that night?"

"No. But he could be anywhere, at the high school, at

his home. Ghosts don't have to hang around this house, you know."

"They sure seem to like to. Maybe it's my grandma. Maybe she's a ghost magnet."

Tom was silent.

"All those kids," I said. "All those kids in this town that go missing, all the time. I think the Stationmaster killed some of them. I think he made them die."

"They're runaways, Ez. They left town, that's all. If what you say is true, there would be dozens and dozens of ghosts."

I set the book on the piano bench. "Not everyone is a ghost, Tom. Even I know that. Some of the dead want other things, easier things, and get them, and go."

His face creased. "What does that mean?"

I flipped through the heavy book, even though the dust flying up made me gag, even though I knew already there was nothing worthwhile in its pages; I had to keep my hands busy. "Clara told me the reason you kissed me."

"Which is why?"

"She said you're just using me to get what you want."

There was a pause. I stopped flipping pages to listen. I could hear the cats mewing somewhere, Martha humming as she scrubbed the stairs.

"What do I want?" Tom asked.

I couldn't answer.

"Clara doesn't know me. Clara's been my sister for a century, and she still doesn't understand anything about me. And she's jealous of you."

I brought my head up. "Why?"

"Because I like you."

He said what I believed, what I thought I knew.

But I had stopped trusting what I knew, years ago, after my parents had died and we were sent to a grandmother we didn't know. We went away from her—and then my sister sent me back; I was always being passed along. Nothing was solid; nothing would stay. How could I trust anything? How could I believe Tom?

"Do you want to know what I want?" Tom said. "Esmé Wong, you know so much about ghosts. Do you know what I want? I want revenge. I want to stop the Stationmaster. I want him to leave. I want him to die. I want him to stay dead. Meeting you—I didn't plan on it. I didn't look for it, and it's not going to do anything for me except make me happy."

"Ghosts can be happy?"

"I hope so."

"Tom, I don't think the Stationmaster will stop. If he's killed before, if he's killed dozens of times, for years ... He's watched people die as a living person, and as a ghost. He's not going to just stop. We have to make him. We need to figure out how to kill him for good, how to kill the dead."

"Simple," Tom said. "Give him what he wants."

The Stationmaster wouldn't come in the house, Mr. Black said. I had never even seen him on the platform of the train station, only on the tracks. Ghosts haunted different places, Tom said—sometimes the places where they had died, sometimes places that held deep memories for them. I wondered if my grandmother knew these things. I wondered if she could have just told me.

I asked Tom, "How long did you live with the Stationmaster before ..."

"We died?" Clara said. "You think you could speak aloud it by now. *Died*. We died. It's not like it should be a surprise. It's not like it's catching."

"Five years for me," Tom said, ignoring Clara. "I was twelve when I was adopted. Seventeen when I died. And three years for Clara. She was adopted at ten."

Clara put a hand over her eyes dramatically. "And now I'll be thirteen forever."

"That explains some things about you," I said. "Ten and twelve, that's kind of old to be adopted. Is that why the Stationmaster took you? Because everyone else wanted babies?"

"There weren't too many babies on the train," Tom said, "even though they called them that, the baby trains. But there were much younger children and healthier-looking children and children that ..." he faltered, "showed better."

"What do you mean?"

"They put us on stages. At each station, they set up a stage, the Children's Aid Society workers, and they told us to behave and look nice and be special."

"Be special?"

"Some kids sang to get attention or danced."

"Show-offs," Clara muttered.

"I didn't," Tom said. "I was sad. I missed my father. I couldn't smile."

"I was angry," Clara said. "A woman tried to carry me off in her arms. Carry me! At ten. I screamed and bit her hand. After that, it was hard to get adopted."

"You had a father?" I asked Tom. "A real one?"

"We weren't all orphans."

We were sitting on the front porch, waiting for sunset, for the darkness and moonrise that would bring the Stationmaster. Tom fell silent. Clara caught one of the cats. When she tried to curl its long pointed ear around a twig, the cat swatted her, hissing, and I stood. "I'm going to get dinner."

Clara tossed the twig away. "Oh, the living. Always having to stop and eat."

"Clara, do you want anything?" I said. "Some candy maybe?"

She made a face and let the cat escape. Tom grinned at me. In the kitchen, I took a package of instant noodles from the pantry, and opened it over a bowl. I added water and stirred the goopy mixture. I wished someone had taught me how to cook before I became invisible. I put the bowl in the microwave and pushed the buttons. I heard the microwave whirl and turn on.

And then I heard whistling.

Every muscle in my body tensed. It was twilight. The dogcatcher was not coming back this late. And I had heard only one other person whistle in this town. One ghost.

There was the door at the back of the kitchen, the locked door that led to nothing, only the sharp drop-off of the hill outside—one of the Builder's follies, I knew now. The door to nowhere was always locked. And through its window, I saw the Stationmaster walking up the hill.

"Shh."

I turned, my heart thudding. A man stood in the doorway of the kitchen, a man I had never seen before. He was plump, wearing a suit that threatened to burst its buttons. He had a thick brown mustache that turned up on the ends, twisted with wax. His sleeves were rolled to his elbows, and something poked up from his breast pocket, some kind of a tool, a ruler or plane. The man reached into his vest pocket, and took out a watch on a long gold chain.

"You're the Builder," I said.

He shushed me again. He raised a finger to his lips, then pointed at the door that led to nowhere.

I didn't look at it. "He's not supposed to come in the house," I said. "He's not allowed. Mr. Black said he never lived here in life, so he's not allowed."

The Builder shook his head. He was pointing at the fireplace now. "Up," he said.

The fireplace was cold and dark. I had never really noticed it before, beside the big stove, which I also never gave a second glance to (my grandmother had a microwave, after all). There was a wide, empty hearth, the chimney blackened by years of soot.

"Are you kidding?" I said. "I can't go up there. I'm not a ghost."

The whistling sounded louder now; he was right under the door. Was he floating? Could he fly?

"Up," the Builder whispered.

The knob was rattling, starting to turn. The door to nowhere wasn't locked anymore.

I went in the chimney. I went first, ducking under the mantle and stepping into the hearth. The dark sides of the chimney closed in around me. I tried not to breathe the ash and soot and spider webs. I remembered the tunnel, the secret passageway under the kiln. Then the Builder was beside me, in the way that ghosts were, pointing.

"Up," he said.

My eyes adjusted. Above me, I could see bricks jutting out, making holds for my feet and hands. At the very top of the chimney burned a small square of light. I hesitated.

But then I heard the sound of a door creaking, a door that hadn't been opened in years.

A voice called out into the kitchen, "Little girl? Little girl?"

Bits of ash broke from the brick, crumbling under my fingers as I climbed. The soot stung my eyes so I closed them

131

and began to rise by feel. I became aware that the Builder had passed me somehow; he was at the top. Then we both were. It was light again, a fading light, and he was pulling me out of the chimney, heaving me out onto the roof, onto a flat, wide expanse, hemmed by a railing. The widow's walk. The air felt clear and cold. I coughed and breathed in. I stood and could see the green tops of trees, the road, the empty yard in twilight. I couldn't see Tom or Clara. They must have been sitting on the porch right below us.

My arms were gray with soot. I held them out before me, and realized I was shaking. "How did he do that?" I asked. "How could the Stationmaster come into the house? Mr. Black said he couldn't."

"He couldn't come into the house in *life*," the Builder said, standing politely beside me. "He had no place here, no reason to come inside. We would have called the constable had he just waltzed into our home then." He chuckled. "But that was in life, of course. The dead may do as they wish."

"What do you mean?"

"The dead may come and go. The dead have no timetable, no restrictions, no rules, though many hold fast to the ones they had in life."

Always building, Mr. Black had said.

"What if the Stationmaster comes up here? What if he climbs the chimney?"

But the Builder shook his head. "He won't come up here."

"Why?"

"I don't hear him whistling anymore. Do you? And you, my dear," he smiled at me. "You should be getting down as well."

"Esmé Wong!"

I inched to the railing and looked down.

Martha stood in the yard, glaring up at me, her hands on her hips. "Get down here this instant! What did I tell you about the roof!"

The Builder came to stand beside me. "Miss Moore," he said, dipping his head. If he had been wearing a hat, he would have removed it. Instead, he took the pocket watch out from his vest, looped on a long gold chain.

In the yard, Martha dropped her hands. Her face looked strange.

"It's early evening," the Builder said, studying the watch. "Not my usual time. And I like to be punctual. I like to keep a schedule, whenever possible. The house will be done soon, you know. Because we've stuck to a schedule."

"I've heard that," I said.

"She'll be a beauty. You'll see." He put his watch back in his pocket. He smiled at me. And then he fell off the roof.

It was Tom who found the way down, found the ladder propped on the side of the house. The Builder was always leaving ladders around, Tom said; you could never tell where you were going to find one.

By the time I reached the last rung, the Builder was gone, but everyone still stood around in a circle, looking down, as if he lay crumpled in the grass before them. Even Clara was quiet. Martha cried soundlessly.

He wanted to finish the house. That was what the Builder wanted. I knew that without having to ask.

"Avoid the place of your death," Mr. Black said. "Avoid it at all costs."

"I know," I said, as though it applied to me. "So why did he do it then? Why did he go on the roof? Why didn't he just send me up by myself? Why go with me?"

"It's a pull," Tom said. "An irresistible pull. You want it—and you think it will be different this time. You think you can make it better."

Martha looked at me. Her face was puffy, and her eyes had turned to slits. "I would if I could have, wouldn't I? If I had known, wouldn't I have done something?"

"Martha," I said. "What are you talking about?"

She turned without another word and ran into the house. We watched her go. She disappeared around the corner and I heard a door slam.

"I don't understand. What did I do?"

"Martha feels bad," Tom said. "About the—" He indicated the ground, the ground where nothing lay. "About *him*."

"Still? She feels bad after a century?"

"Martha feels a lot of things," Clara said. "A lot."

"Quit it, you," Mr. Black said.

But Clara kept going. "Love, for instance. Martha feels love."

I stared at her. Clara had never smiled at me quite like that before, her upper lip curling over her teeth. Except when she had lied to me about Tom.

"Jealousy," Clara said, her eyes dancing. "Envy. Lust." She looked at me like I was in on a secret, a secret she wanted to share with me, and keep from the others.

But the others all knew.

"I said, quit," Mr. Black said.

"Clara," Tom said.

"What is it?" I asked. "Who does Martha love? What are you talking about?"

Clara grinned and bit her lip. Her eyes moved ever so slightly to the ladder.

"The *Builder*? Martha is in love with the Builder?"

"Was in love," Mr. Black said.

"But he's old," I said.

"Not that old," Tom said.

"He has a mustache." I thought of his checkered vest, his pocket watch. "He's a buffoon."

"Thank you," Mr. Black said.

"And he's *married*." I looked up at the ladder, as if Xavier Vale still stood there, hammering, as if I could hold him accountable. "Did he ever …?"

"No," Tom said.

"No, no, no," Mr. Black said.

"But she wanted to," Clara said.

I wanted to go after Martha, but I knew I wouldn't find her, not if she didn't want to be found. In my head, I traced the path Martha had run. I pictured her rounding the corner of the house, pictured the door that went into … "The kitchen!" I said. "Martha went in the kitchen. She never goes there."

"She did," Clara said, "when she died."

CHAPTER 13

Dance or Die

That night, Mr. Black sat with me in my darkened bedroom, watching over me while I pretended to sleep. But I was wide awake. I wanted to talk with him about Martha, but he wouldn't say anything more. In the darkness, I heard sips and gulps and sloshing.

At midnight, Clara came to relieve Mr. Black. I couldn't sleep with her there, leering at me from the shadows. I didn't even pretend to. She hummed as she skirted my room, touching things. I heard the sound of my closet door opening. I heard the slide of hangers as she looked through my clothes.

Finally I said, "I'd sleep better if you left."

She did. I dreamed that Martha came and sat on the end of my bed like she used to. I dreamed that she smoothed my hair and said to me, "It's not your fight. It's not your death."

But it was my fight. And it would—it might be—my death too.

The Stationmaster would hurt me if I didn't stop him. He would hunt me. He could come into my grandmother's house. He was following me, looking for me. He could kill me.

"Why him?" I said aloud in my sleep.

"Ez?" And then Tom was peering over me. "Ez, did you say something?"

I sat up. Tom sat on the edge of the bed, leaning over me. I pulled the covers up, over my thin white T-shirt. What was I wearing? Some ridiculous cast-off of my sister's.

And Tom was looking at it. "Are you a dancer?" he asked.

I looked down at my T-shirt. *DANCE OR DIE* it read in flaking, red letters. Great. "No. My sister is. Was. She quit. It's a long story, but she has a real job now, making real money, and she seems to be happy about it. So."

"You have a sister? Is she invisible too?"

"Not that I know of." I smiled a little to think of the Firecracker invisible, barreling down subway platforms and sidewalks, pushing surprised people out of the way. She would take advantage of being invisible, in the way Clara said I should have.

"Why isn't she here?" Tom said. "Why doesn't she live here with you?"

"It's complicated."

"Everything is complicated," Tom said.

"She doesn't want to live here, I guess. She doesn't want to be a mom to me on top of everything else she has to do. She did it when our mom and dad died. She held everything together then. But I guess it got to be too much. I guess *I* got to be too much."

Tom nodded. "My father didn't want to be a father after my mother died. He was a decent man. Was. After she died, he was like Mr. Black, though." He reached to the floor beside the bed, and held up a bottle, one of the empties Mr. Black left in his wake like breadcrumbs.

"Oh," I said.

137

"He drank like Mr. Black. But worse."

"Worse?" I was always tripping over those empties, pitching them into the recycling, only to find, the next time I passed the bin, the bottles were gone. They had vanished, like Martha's stitches.

The work of the dead.

"Mr. Black is ashamed of himself," Tom said. "My father wasn't. And when he drank, he got angry. He drank more and more, got angrier and angrier. He lost his job. So I got a job: selling papers in the street in the morning, and shining shoes at night. Stealing a little. I stole, Ez. I stole food."

I remembered the apple. "I know," I said.

"Then a woman from a charity came up to me in the street one day, and asked if I would like to go to California. They grew oranges there, she said."

"But you didn't go to California."

"We went west. That much was true. We went west and left New York."

"Only to Pennsylvania."

"The woman was nice," he insisted. "She bought a paper from me. She didn't know then who would adopt me, that he would be worse than my real father. No one did. And they wouldn't have let him take us if they had known."

"What was it like with the Stationmaster?" I asked.

"We hardly saw anyone, all those years. He made us stay inside or on the property, close to the shack. We didn't go to school, even. Clara can't read. I learned before, but she never did." Tom was sitting close to me, close enough so I could smell the earth on him. It didn't scare me away. "Ez," Tom said, "what Clara said before about me—it isn't true. It isn't. What I want is revenge. I want to stop the Stationmaster."

"I know," I said.

"I would never do anything to hurt you. Or take advantage of you, or ..."

"I know. I know that now."

"I want revenge for myself, and now that he hurt you—Ez, I want revenge for you too."

Tom was so close I could see myself in his eyes, a girl in an old T-shirt. I was visible. I was alive in his eyes.

I was dreaming.

I had slept in snatches, dreaming the old dream: my mother dancing on a dark stage. The sun streamed over my bed when I finally woke, well into mid-morning. The sheets were swirled, my legs pulled free of covers, bare and exposed. And the chair across from the bed looked rumpled, dented, as though still holding the shape of the one who had left it. Tom. I pictured him sitting there, awake all night.

Instinctively, I pulled my T-shirt down over my knees. The light through the windows was bright, but I yawned and stretched and would have pulled the quilt up and gone back to sleep, except a voice drifted in from the front doors and up the stairs.

"Esmé!"

I knew that voice. That voice got me out of bed on a regular basis, and told me I was going to be late, and reprimanded me when I was; I always was.

That voice belonged to my sister.

"Esmé Wong, where the heck are you?"

I heard the crash of the front doors slamming, the thud of something heavy being set down. The Firecracker was here. The Firecracker had come to Wellstone, Pennsylvania, to our grandmother's house. The Firecracker was downstairs.

I raced into the closet, and fumbled for clothes. I was wearing my sister's shirt, which I had probably stolen. She was going to kill me for that. I yanked jeans over my legs, pausing as I realized: my sister wasn't going to be able to see my shirt. She wasn't going to be able to see anything about me.

I had bigger problems.

"Esmé!"

I darted into the hallway, and leaned over the banister. I saw the top of a head, glossy black hair. My sister paced the downstairs hall, hands on her hips, a huge suitcase slumped at her side. I tiptoed down the stairs, one step at a time.

I had learned to be almost soundless—my grandmother never seemed to hear me, anyway. But a stair squeaked and my sister said, "What was that?"

Had she heard my footstep, actually heard me?

She was swatting at something, a Manx. "Stupid cat. Get off my bag, you stupid cat. Esmé! Where the heck?" She looked up. She met my eyes, looked right at me.

"Hi," I said.

She looked away, toward the sitting room. "Esmé?"

"I'm right here."

She tilted her head the other way, toward the dining room. "Esmé? Seriously, this is a huge house. You have to come down here and get me."

"I am here," I said. "I'm right in front of you. I'm on the staircase."

She turned her head slowly, her eyes scanning the steps. I saw her look for me and not see me. I saw her frown and scan the hall. Then I reached out and touched her arm.

She flinched, flinging me off. "Spider web! Cat!"

"No. It's me. It's Esmé. I'm here. I'm right here. You can hear me."

"But I can't *see* you. Where are you?" She stuck her arm out wildly and slapped me in the stomach.

"Ow," I said.

She brought her hand back around. She connected with me, feeling my arms, my shoulders. "It's you," she said.

"I've been trying and trying to tell you."

"What happened to you?"

"I told you. I told you on the phone." I took a deep breath. "I'm invisible."

My sister yanked her arm in, as if I had bitten her. She spoke to the air, to a spot beside my head. "That's not funny, Esmé. I don't know how you're doing this. I don't know what Grandma taught you."

"What Grandma *taught* me?"

"But you need to quit this right now."

"I'd love to," I said. "I would really love to. I really wish I could stop doing this." I kicked her suitcase. "And this." I pulled her ponytail, her head dipping back. She swatted at me and missed. "I wish I didn't look like this." I caught the Manx still sniffing around the Firecracker's suitcase, and picked it up, rocking the cat in my arms.

The Firecracker backed up until she hit the wall, staring at the floating cat. "What have you done?" she whispered.

"Nothing. When I got off the train from New York, I was like this. I was invisible. No one saw me at school. Grandma didn't see me at the station. She hasn't seen me once."

"But she knows," the Firecracker said. "She knows something is wrong. She said something happened, but she wouldn't tell me on the phone. Why aren't you talking to her?"

"I can't," I said. "I've been calling her name, leaving her messages. I can't make her hear me. So far, you're the only living person that can."

"*Living* person? What do you mean? Oh!" She brought her hands up to her mouth. "Oh Esmé, are you dead?"

"No!" I said. "Why does everyone keep asking me that?"

"You hit your head. You hit your head when you went into the subway tunnel. You blacked out. You had a concussion, they said, and they said to watch you. What if I didn't watch you long enough? What if you died on the train, or at the station?"

"No," I said. "No, I can feel pain. I can feel hot and cold. I'm hungry. I'm thirsty. I still eat and sleep. I bleed. Ghosts can't do that."

"Right," my sister nodded.

I narrowed my eyes. "How do you know all that?"

"Esmé, are you naked?

"Excuse me?" I said. "*No.*"

"Why are your clothes invisible then? Are you wearing my clothes?"

"Look, I don't know the rules, okay? My clothes are invisible. Things I write are invisible. I tried to write a letter to Grandma, and—"

"Don't change the subject. When you left, I had more than a few outfits missing."

"My word," a voice said. "The resemblance is extraordinary. Are all the living this annoying, or just you and your family?" Mr. Black sat on the staircase, peering at us through the bottom of a bottle.

"Get out of here," I said.

"What?" the Firecracker said.

"I'm not talking to you."

"Oh," Mr. Black said. "So you wanted me to guard you last night. You wanted my protection in the dark, but in the cold light of morning, you don't want me around. You're tired of old Mr. Black. You're too embarrassed to introduce him to your family."

He was drunk. More than usual. I wondered if it was Martha that had put him out, Martha crying over the Builder, Martha running into the kitchen, Martha … Mr. Black drained the bottle and lobbed it at me. I ducked and he missed, the bottle tumbling over the stairs, knocking into my sister's suitcase.

"Ignore it," I said. "It's just a ghost."

"I know," the Firecracker said.

"You know?" I stared at my sister. "You *know*? How can you know? What do you mean you know?"

"Never mind," the Firecracker said. She bent to her suitcase.

"Can you see him?" I pointed to Mr. Black—as if my sister could see me point.

He gave a little wave. "Hello," he said cheerfully.

"Can you see a drunk ghost on the stairs, right now?" I said.

"Drunk?" the Firecracker said. "A drunk ghost? That's a good one." She righted her suitcase, slinging her huge purse over her shoulder.

"You do hear him, right?" I said.

"No, I don't."

"Yes, you do."

"No, I don't."

"You do! You do!" Mr. Black said delightedly, clapping his hands. "She does."

"She does not," my sister said.

We all stopped what we were doing, my sister fiddling with the bags, Mr. Black clapping. "You see ghosts," I said softly to the Firecracker. "You hear them."

She didn't look at me. "I don't want to talk about it. I'm not talking about it with you. Not now." She started up the steps with her bags. "Where am I staying?"

"Staying?" I trailed after her. "You're staying?"

"You're a truant and apparently invisible. Grandma's house is overrun with cats and junk, and she thinks you're dead. Yes, I'm staying."

Mr. Black leaned out of her way, but she glided past him effortlessly, as if she really did see him there on the stairs. I couldn't make up my mind about her, if she was pretending or lying or what. "How long are you staying?" I asked. "What about your job?"

She stopped and turned to me or tried to, looking somewhere above my head. "I got laid off. There's not a big call for publicists right now. I don't have a job anymore."

I reached out for my sister's arm, and she jumped. The touch must have felt like it came out of nowhere, must have been frightening. *I* must have been frightening. "I'm sorry," I said.

She shrugged. "I can't afford the apartment in New York without a job. So..."

"We lost the apartment?" I changed my voice. "I hated that apartment."

"Just find me a room, please," the Firecracker said. "One without cats."

I sat on the bed of the room the Firecracker had chosen, the blue room, watching my sister unpack her suitcase. "I think Grandma thinks I'm dead," I said. "Grandma's kind of strange. She goes places at night."

"It's not that strange," the Firecracker said. "People work the night shift."

"I know that," I said. "She works at a nursing home. But she goes other places. She has other jobs. She ... freelances."

"How do you know this?"

"I followed her once. I'm invisible, remember? I can do those kinds of things."

"Esmé Wong, I'd better not hear that you're shoplifting."

I sat up straighter. "Listen to me. Grandma went to a house. A haunted house. She has this ability ..." I paused. "She hears ghosts, I think. Those people in the house she went to hired her to hear their ghost and get rid of it. She's got this big black bag, and she's got candles and dowsing rods and prayer books."

"Look," the Firecracker said. "Let's slow down."

"She's got dowsing rods and five hundred cats," I said. "She picked up my voice on a tape recorder. I met the ghost in the house we went to, and Grandma knew what the ghost wanted."

"You met a ghost?" the Firecracker said. "Already?" She sank onto the bed next to me. *On* me, actually. I squealed and she moved over. "Sorry. Tell me when it started."

"When what started?" I asked.

"When you started being able to sense the ghosts."

I looked at the Firecracker. I tried to study her face, but she had made her face into a mask. She looked hard, older than she actually was. For the first time, I realized that reminded me of Clara. What would happen to you to make you have to change your face? To make you freeze?

"When I came here," I said, "I got off the train, and the first person I met wasn't a person at all. He was a ghost. Is a ghost. Tom." I waited for my sister to say something, but she didn't, so I kept going. "Well, I guess first I met his sister, Clara. Adopted sister. Anyway, then I met Martha and Mr. Black. And the Stationmaster. I have to warn you about the Stationmaster."

"Wait." The Firecracker held up a hand. "You met all these ghosts. You saw all of them?"

"See them," I said. "All the time. Yes."

"Are any of them here? Right now?"

"No. Mr. Black was on the stairs before. He threw a bottle. You said you knew that."

"I—" The Firecracker looked down at her lap. She messed with something on her black pants, a long white hair. "Stupid cats," she said.

"You can't wear black around here." I thought of Mr. Black. "Unless you're a ghost, then I guess it doesn't show."

"All I have is black." The Firecracker brushed off her pants more urgently.

"Talk to me," I said.

Her eyes stayed fixed on her lap. "Okay. A few days before I turned sixteen, I started having dreams. I dreamed about people, people in my room watching me at night, watching me sleep, people in funny clothes."

"Funny?"

"Like old-fashioned, old. The people weren't scary. They were just … *there*. I kept dreaming about them. And then when I turned sixteen—when I woke up on the morning of my birthday, they were still there in the day."

My voice became very quiet. "What do you mean?"

"I mean, I could still see them, see the people from my dreams standing in my room when I woke up. They weren't dreams, Esmé. They were ghosts. You need to know you're not alone."

"I am alone," I said. "I'm alone and invisible. You left me here."

The mask of her face softened. "I know. I'm sorry. But do you understand? You're not the only one of us to sense ghosts."

"Okay," I said slowly. She was the one who didn't understand. How could I make her know what it was like for

146

me, how real everyone—all the ghosts—were? I didn't make them up. I didn't *think* I saw them. It wasn't a dream. It was every day of my life now. "Did you ever actually talk to your ghosts, the people from your dreams? Did they ever ask things of you?"

The Firecracker frowned. "No. I didn't try to talk to them. I mean, Mom ..."

My body felt slack and cold. "What about Mom?"

"Mom knew about them. Mom experienced them too."

"Mom saw ghosts?"

"Not exactly," the Firecracker said. "She smelled them."

CHAPTER 14

Mr. Black

It was different for everyone, the Firecracker said. All of the women in our family. With her, it was seeing usually, and not always a whole figure. Sometimes, my sister saw snatches of color, a fabric, the corner of a dress. With Mr. Black, the Firecracker said she saw a black cloud, tangled and twisting, like brambles. *His hair*, I thought.

With our mother, it was smells: cinnamon, horses, a cheroot cigar. Grandma could hear things, according to the Firecracker: hooves, cries, fragments of conversation. Grandma called it *cocktail listening*, being half-aware, making herself half-asleep on purpose in order to let the whispers in. She had to concentrate to do it, trance-like. When we moved to live with her, after our parents died, she told the Firecracker that she had heard, as she tucked me into bed one night, a ghost say above my head, *I'm here too*.

"That was why we moved out," the Firecracker said flatly.

I shook my head. "No. We moved out because you turned eighteen, and could take care of me legally. Because we were better off on our own."

It was the Firecracker's turn to shake her head. "No. We moved out because it scared me, what Grandma said. *Grandma* scared me. Mom said we had to hide it, the ghost thing. She said it wasn't a gift. Dancing was a gift. Her gift."

"Your gift too."

"Mom was ashamed of the ghost thing. She didn't really believe in it, even though it happened to her all the time. She thought it was just a quirk, a trait, like … having black hair, or being nearsighted. The Wong women could all sense the dead. It was something to ignore, Mom thought. But Grandma!"

"Grandma makes a living off it," I said. "Or tries to."

"She encouraged it," the Firecracker said. "She kept goading me into things, baiting me, trying to trick me into admitting I saw things, trying to get me to tell her what I saw."

"What did you see?"

She shrugged. "Blue eyes once, I thought. I don't know. I don't really remember."

I tried not to gasp. Had my sister had seen Tom? Had Tom seen me when I was a child? He must have. He had been here all these years. Had he been watching me back then? Had all of them?

When my grandmother saw the Firecracker, there were tears, much fussing and hugging. My grandmother cooked for her, like she used to cook for me when I was a child. I was surprised, when the little mounds of dough on the counter began to take shape as vegetable dumplings and shrimp wontons, to find that I remembered. I remembered her cooking. I remembered the ritual. My grandmother set the dumplings in a pan of boiling oil, lifting them out with a lightweight utensil that had a bamboo handle and a wide webbed basket. I remembered the tool. I remembered the smell of the oil.

I sat behind my sister on the floor of the dining room, behind her chair. I was hungry. There was no mention of me. My grandmother chatted on about the weather, the house, the economy. How she had never liked that city, never understood why my sister wanted to live there. I noticed the tight, clipped tone to my grandmother's voice. She was hiding, chattering on because she was hiding what she really felt and worried about: me. She was barely holding it in.

"I'll steal you something to eat if you ask nice."

I blinked and saw eyes at my level. But not blue eyes. Clara's dark ones glowed under the dining-room table. The tablecloth shrouded the top of her head and hair, making her chest and limbs look disembodied, even more ghostly.

"Shh," I whispered. "Clara, don't ruin everything."

"I haven't had a good scare in such a long while," she said. "Your sister seems susceptible. Vulnerable. *Pretty*, Tom says."

"Stop it," I said. "He did not say that. Stop making things up." I raised myself up on my knees so I could peek across the table. My grandmother looked tired, the skin beneath her eyes creased and gray. Her black hair fell limp, not at all like the springing, set curls I was used to seeing on her. She didn't seem to be eating.

"You know, my work takes me out of the house," she said. "I didn't know how soon, how hard I would have to watch your sister." She fiddled with the silverware, smoothed the tablecloth by her place. "I didn't know how quickly danger would find her. I didn't know what the gift might do to her, where it would take her."

This was too much. I yanked at her napkin. Clara rolled over and began to kick the underside of the table.

"Ghosts," my grandmother said irritably, pulling her napkin back. "This old house. You remember what it's like."

150

"I remember," my sister said.

"It's gotten worse since you left. This one young ghost is particularly disruptive. Touched, I think."

Clara reached toward my grandmother's shoes. I crawled back under the table and slapped her hand. What had my grandmother said about a gift *taking* me someplace? What did she think had happened?

I couldn't stand it. I emerged out from under the table on my grandmother's side.

On the other side of the table, my sister's expression didn't change. She couldn't see me, wasn't looking. She ate without thinking. She ate to avoid speaking, silently chewing, her eyes cast down. My grandmother was looking down too. I stretched my hand toward her.

Then I felt the grip of her fingers around my wrist. My grandmother had reached out and grabbed me.

I was surprised at how strong my grandmother was. With her other hand, she continued holding her chopsticks.

The Firecracker looked up. "Grandma," she said. "Meet Esmé."

My grandmother dropped my wrist. "Esmé," my grandmother said. She was looking down at her plate, looking around the table, looking anywhere but at me. "Esmé."

"She's not dead," the Firecracker said. "And not in limbo or a netherworld. She swears. Just invisible."

Grandmother brought her hands up to her face. I couldn't see her expression from where I stood behind her, but her shoulders were starting to shake. "Esmé," she said. "I thought we had lost you. I thought your gift had come wrong. I thought it had taken you to a dark place."

"What do you mean?" I looked across the table at my sister. "What's going on?"

She put down her chopsticks and swallowed. "It wasn't just for punishment that I sent you here."

"What?" I said numbly.

"It was planned. For when you were sixteen. But you started having trouble earlier, getting in trouble earlier, seeing things much sooner than we expected—"

"What do you mean, *we*?"

"Grandma and I thought you should come here because … because it went so badly with me, when I turned sixteen, when my gift came. Mom didn't warn me, not really, and then she died, and I didn't know what to do, what was happening. I tried to hide it, deny it."

"You were still denying it this morning," I said.

"I was waiting for Grandma to tell you."

"But she can't even hear me!"

"Try," the Firecracker said. She leaned across the table. If she could have seen my hand to hold it, I know she would have. "Try again, Esmé."

"Do you hear me?" I asked. I crouched before my grandmother. I put my hand on the table next to her. "Grandma, can you hear me talking?"

"Faintly," my grandmother said. "A whisper. Far away."

Why was she having trouble? The Firecracker heard me fine. "I'm right next to you."

"Wait," my grandmother said. She closed her eyes. "Speak again."

I closed my own eyes. I thought of my grandmother. I hardly knew her at all. I remembered her from when I was a child as distant, foreboding. I remembered her more as pieces, as objects: a car motor at night; a match striking a candle; a big black bag; a mason jar of nettles; a stinking pot of boiling, almond-shaped leaves. But she and my sister were all I had. What if my sister complained about her so much because she was scared of what my grandmother could do, what my sister herself had been turning into? What if my grandmother wasn't weird or a witch?

What if I was just like her?

I took a breath. "Grandma. It's me, Esmé. I'm here. I've been here for weeks, in the house. I've met all your ghosts." I struggled with what to say. "They're very nice."

"Mostly," my grandmother said with her eyes closed.

"Do you want me to tell you about them? You've been hearing them for years. Do you want to know their names, their stories?"

"No," my grandmother said. "I want to know about you."

There was nothing in my grandmother's books about someone like me, someone invisible, though she had been looking for weeks, since I first failed to show up at the train station, she said. Now we looked together, riffling through pages, dislodging envelopes of dried herbs and bookmarks of feathers. In the middle of searching, my sister got a funny look on her face.

"Blue eyes," she said. "I see blue eyes."

I turned. Tom stood in the doorway.

I surveyed the sitting room, what he must have thought of the mess we had made. Here I was with my family, more of my family than had been together for a very long time.

I looked at him shyly. "Hi," I said.

"Hi."

"We're trying to figure out what's up with me. Why I'm invisible. So far, we've got: stayed too long in the subway tunnel, hit my head, terrible illness ..."

"Terrible illness?"

"And, last but not least, the most promising theory: something is wrong with my gift."

He paused. "Your gift?"

"That's what my grandmother calls it. My sister calls it a curse, still. But Grandma thinks we should use what we have, the Wong women." I took a breath. This was hard to say. "I guess every woman in my family can sense ghosts. Somehow. Apparently. Apparently it starts when we turn sixteen—always, as far back as my grandmother can remember. But everyone gets the gift a little differently. My grandmother hears things, mostly. My sister mostly sees things."

"What?" my sister said, looking around. "What's going on?"

"And you?" Tom said. "What do you do? What's your gift?"

"I don't know for sure yet. Mine came early. And it came wrong."

"It made you invisible to the living."

"I guess."

"It's not just that you can see the dead," Tom said. "They're the only ones that can see *you*. Is that your gift?"

"I don't think so." I darted a look at my grandmother, by the bookshelf. Could she hear us? "Grandma thinks it happened early to me because it's extra strong. She thinks it's thrown things off—thrown me off. It's *so* strong, my body doesn't know what to do, so my body just … faded. I turned off."

"The young man," my grandmother said. She was speaking to my sister as she filed books away, not even looking at Tom and me. "He's in the doorway. That's the blue you see. He's a good man. Good strong voice."

"Thanks," Tom said. To me he whispered, "I didn't know she could hear us."

I shook my head. "Sometimes, I guess."

"All the time," my grandmother said.

"The eyes are moving," my sister said.

Tom slid onto the piano bench beside me. I resisted the urge to touch him, to lean my face close so that he might touch me. I didn't know for sure how much my sister could see or my grandmother could hear.

For the first time in weeks, I felt horribly, obviously visible.

"Amazing," Tom said. "Between the three of you, you could start a business."

"I already have a business," my grandmother said. "Successful, thank you very much."

Silently, Tom made a face at me; I wondered if the Firecracker could see that. But I made a face back at him, sticking out my tongue. He snorted a laugh, and I composed myself. "Grandma?" I said. "It's a little crowded in here. We're going to go outside, okay?"

"Fine," my grandmother said. "Be back before dark. And stay away from the pond."

Tom took my hand. As we walked through the doorway I heard my sister ask, "What's wrong with the pond?"

And then we were running, leaping down the front stairs, into the evening. I felt like light. I felt like I could run as fast as Tom; I could disappear and reappear and glide the way he did.

He picked a spot on the grass to sit down and I reclined beside him. "I never thought ghosts might feel free before," I said. "But it is. It's freeing, being invisible."

"Especially when people can hear you," Tom said.

"Yes, that's true."

"Especially when you know you're not alone."

"I know," I said. I watched his face. We lay in the grass while the clouds above us changed from gold to gray and purple, the light in Tom's eyes dimming as the sun dipped.

155

He touched my face. It was like an electric shock sparking through me. Though the temperature around me was dropping, my body hummed with heat. When the sky turned navy-colored, I could see flashes of black, wings dipping and gliding above the tops of trees.

"Bats," Tom said, and when I stiffened, "It's all right. They can't run into us. They're such good navigators."

"Even though we're invisible?"

"Even though."

I sat up. "Tom, bats see you. Cats see you. Do all animals see ghosts?"

"It seems like it. Haven't you ever been around a cat that hissed for no reason, or a dog that barked at something that wasn't there?"

"Yes," I said. "That happens a lot around here. Tom, you've been here, close to my grandmother's house, for years, right?"

"Since I died."

"How often did the house change hands?"

Tom said. "After the Builder died, then Martha and Mr. Black, the Vale family moved out. The house was empty for a long time. Stories started then, stories of how it was haunted. But people always talked, even when the house was being built, about the land, about how long the construction was taking, about how many problems it had. After the deaths, a couple moved in and then out again—some distant relatives of the Builder's. They said the house was cursed."

"Clara probably didn't help," I said.

"But when your grandmother moved in, she wasn't scared. She wasn't frightened by stories, or Clara. She's stayed for a long time."

"I lived here," I said quietly. "I lived here when I was a little girl, me and my sister." I looked up at him. "Do you remember us? Do you remember *me*? I had long hair, like I do now."

"You were very sad," Tom said. "We left you alone."

"What does that mean?"

"I mean, I wouldn't let Clara bother you. I mean, Martha stayed out of your way, and Mr. Black was on his very best behavior around you and your sister. We knew something was the matter, something was making you sad."

"How do you remember all this?"

"I remember. It wasn't that long ago for me, you know. Just ten years, and I've been around for a hundred. I watched you when you were little," he said. "You were always strong and brave, even then."

"Why didn't you say anything when I came back here?" I demanded.

"I didn't know it was you at first."

"Well, once you did. Why didn't you say anything?"

"I didn't want to scare you," Tom said. "A beau who's a ghost is bad enough, never mind one that's a century old, one that knew you when you were a child, one you wouldn't even remember."

"A beau?" I said.

"A young man. A caller. A—"

"Boyfriend," I said.

He grinned. "Yes, that."

I don't know what I might have said in response. I saw him smile at me, but then his smile fell away. His eyes darkened, as if a shadow had passed over him. He wasn't looking at me, wasn't seeing me anymore. He was staring back at the house, at my grandmother. My grandmother stood out on the front porch, scanning the yard, seeing no one, and screaming.

Tom and I ran to her. She flinched as we pounded invisibly up the front steps. I took her hands quickly. "Grandma," I said loudly. "Grandma, it's Esmé. I'm right in front of you."

Her eyes focused, settling on a spot nearby.

"Tom is here too. The young man. What's going on?"

"She's gone," my grandmother said. "She's gone."

"What's happening? Who is?"

"I heard whistling. That was all. Whistling."

"Stay here, Grandma," I said. Tom was already running; I ran too, down the steps and across the yard, after him.

The Stationmaster had taken her, taken my sister.

I tried to call out to Tom, but I couldn't breathe and form words at the same time. I couldn't run this hard for long, not all the way to the station. I would never catch a ghost. Already, I felt a stitch in my side. I slowed. Then I saw the cat.

I nearly ran into it, a gray lump in the yard right in front of me. There were more cats standing over the yard. The Manxes, a herd of them. They all faced the same direction, looking at something. And they were all hissing.

"Tom!"

But he was gone across the street, far ahead. I turned back to the cats. They stared at the house, though I could see nothing unusual. My grandmother had gone back inside. The front porch steps stood empty, except for cats. More cats were rooted on the path that led to the backyard. They stood frozen, staring. What were they looking at? I backtracked up the hill and followed the path, turning into the backyard. More cats in the backyard. More cats staring at the pond.

And in front of the pond: the Stationmaster waited.

I said, "What did you do with my sister?"

The Stationmaster grinned. His smile was gray.

"Give me my sister," I said. "Bring her back. She won't fall for your tricks. She won't die for you. She's strong."

The Stationmaster took a step—just one step—forward, and I could smell the earth on him, the decay stronger than on any of the other ghosts. I looked around wildly for a weapon. I saw the garden hose curled at the spigot, a bathtub rusting against the side of the house.

"You're wild," the Stationmaster said. "You and your sister. You got no parents."

"I've got my grandmother," I said.

Was she watching from the windows? Could she hear this?

"You got no manners."

"That's true," I said. I grabbed the only thing I could find, a pebble on the path. I lobbed it at him and ran. He ducked and lunged for me. The cats unfroze and scattered. I would run around the house, and down to the road. I would get help. I would get Tom.

But I heard, rather than saw, the lantern: the creak of the handle as he swung it, the sighing of the rusted joints. I turned just in time to see a red flash as he brought it over his head. The glass in the lantern was a deep red, an iron red, reflecting his face as if it floated in a pool of blood. The glass caught the flashes of what early stars were out already; caught his terrible look of concentration, forehead lined, teeth dug into his lips.

I reacted instinctively. I caught the lantern in my hands, stopping the blow to my head. But the force knocked me backward, and the heat of the burning lantern shocked me, searing my hands. I cried out, but didn't drop it. I stumbled back, then looked down in surprise. There was water around my ankles.

I was standing in the pond.

"Come on, wild cat," the Stationmaster said. He began to walk into the water toward me. "Can you swim?"

I backed up as he approached, sinking deeper and deeper into the water, which swirled around my shins, then knees, brown and cold. I gripped the lantern by its handle, which was not hot. I dipped one burned hand, the worse one, into the water, and said through gritted teeth, "What did those kids ever do to you? Why do you need to hurt kids?"

The Stationmaster kept coming. "Children should be seen and not heard. You need discipline," the Stationmaster said. "Manners." He was moving steadily toward me through the water.

The mud beneath my feet was soft, catching at my sneakers, pulling me down. My clothes were getting heavy; I was up to my waist in water. The lantern handle cut into my seared hand, but I held fast to it. "What do you want?" I asked the Stationmaster.

"Discipline," the Stationmaster said. "Manners."

"What do you *want*?" I was up to my chest in water.

"Supervision." The Stationmaster leapt across the pond.

It was leaping, like flying. No splash. No sound at all. In no time he had crossed the water separating us, and lunged for the lantern with one hand. With the other, he pushed my head, shoving me down into the water.

All I saw was brown. All I felt was water streaming into my eyes, my nose—his hand, a weight on my head. I shook and flailed. I let go of the lantern, and the pressure on my head released. I shot up to the surface of the water, gasping. He stood over me while I floundered for a foothold, my sneakers sinking in mud. The water was too deep; I was too short.

The Stationmaster raised his lantern.

Behind his shoulder, I saw something move near the house. Mr. Black stood on the second story balcony, watching me.

"Help!" I said. I waved my arms.

A whistle as the lantern sliced through air. I ducked under the water, pushing myself as deep as I could, and the lantern hit the surface above me with a mute splash. I hadn't had time to take a full breath, and I popped back up to the surface, sputtering.

The Stationmaster dragged the lantern through the water. Again, there wasn't time to breathe. I darted a glance toward the balcony as I pushed myself beneath the surface.

Mr. Black was gone.

Another crash above me. Bubbles flooded through the water. I could open my eyes, but I couldn't see anything; the pond was as brown as earth. I forced myself to stay down and kicked. My lungs burned and my legs in their jeans felt so heavy. When I shot back up to the surface, I had swum into the center of the pond.

Mr. Black stood on the bank.

I thrashed and treaded water. "Help me, Mr. Black. You've got to help me."

The Stationmaster turned. "Black," he said. "A hopeless case. You were from the poorhouse, weren't you, boy?"

"I—," Mr. Black stammered. "I—"

"I can always tell. Drunkenness is a sickness, poisons the blood of the mother. You were from bad blood, weren't you? Inferior stock. You hadn't a chance."

Mr. Black paced the bank.

I treaded, gasping as I spoke. "Mr. Black, help. He's going to kill me."

"I can't!" Mr. Black said. "I can't go in there. You know that."

"Please."

"No," Mr. Black moaned. "Not again."

The water was rippling, moving in wider and wider waves toward me as the Stationmaster waded closer, speaking steadily, like a chant, "Discipline. Manners."

I tried to breathe, tried to summon my strength to swim.

But when I raised my arms, I felt pain in my head, slicing through me. The Stationmaster was holding my hair. He had grabbed my long ponytail, sending knives of pain into my scalp and down my neck. I screamed. He looped my hair around his wrist like a rope. He yanked me toward him through the water.

"Mr. Black!" I screamed.

Water filled my mouth.

"Discipline. Manners." The words close to my head. The smell like death. "Supervision."

Release. The pain left me.

My hair was free, floating in the water. Only a dull pounding in my head and in my hands. There was water in my nose, water in my eyes. I fought to reach the other side of the pond, hauling myself through the cattails. I collapsed onto the bank, coughing. I was freezing and dirty. I tasted something salty in my mouth, and spit. Blood ran down the side of my face, a river coming from my scalp.

I wanted to lie down. I wanted to sleep. But I forced myself to stand, shaking and dripping. I forced myself to look at the pond. There was no sign of the Stationmaster.

But a man in black floated facedown in the water.

"Thank you," I whispered to Mr. Black. "Thank you."

CHAPTER 15

The Lower Vale

After I had been cleaned up; after Martha had run a hot bath and helped me get into it, peeling off my muddy clothes while I shivered, teeth chattering; after I had been wrapped in a blanket and my burns bandaged; after my grandmother had made hot drinks for all of us, even Tom and Clara and Martha, setting places for them, even though she couldn't see them—we sat around the kitchen table and waited.

Tom said there was no sign of my sister at the station. Clara said she had checked the tunnel under the house; Martha, the woods and fields. My sister was nowhere. My sister was gone.

I couldn't stop shivering, though I was no longer cold.

"She's not dead," my grandmother said.

"How do you know?" I whispered.

"Because I can't *sense* her. Can you? Try, Esmé. If she had passed on, you would know. You would feel her."

I concentrated for a moment. "No." But I didn't know what that would feel like.

"Ghosts can't hurt the living," my grandmother said. "Except ..." she paused. "Except for people like us, women like us, who can sense ghosts."

"Have you ever been hurt by a ghost, Grandma?"

She nodded. "But only a few times over many years. Scratched. Bruised. Pushed against a wall. Pushed down a staircase."

"Who did *that*?"

"Someone who was very sad, and very lonely, and very tired of not being heard."

"I heard the Stationmaster," I said. "I heard him loud and clear. *Manners*, he said."

"*Discipline*," Clara said.

"*Supervision*," Tom said.

"If you give ghosts what they want, they disappear."

"That's true," my grandmother said, surprised to hear me say it.

"But I can't give him what he wants," I said. "He wants to hurt more kids. He wants more people to die for him. I can't let that happen, so I can't make him go."

"No one is saying you have to make him go, Esmé," my grandmother said kindly, though she was speaking to a teacup.

"I hear *and* see him. I feel him. I'm the only one of us who can."

"Your sister is just out of practice," my grandmother said. "She'll come home and then we'll ... then we'll ..." Her voice trailed off. She set her cup down without drinking any.

"There's a reason I'm invisible. I know you think it's a mistake, my gift coming much too soon, coming wrong. But I think it's sharpened everything. I can see ghosts, hear them, touch them—"

"Touch them?" Clara smirked.

Martha kicked her under the table.

"I can hurt them," I said. "I know I can do that."

"But he's already dead, Ez," Tom spoke up. "Even if you hurt the Stationmaster, even if you kill him, what's that going to do? He's already dead."

"Well, dying again is not pleasant."

We all turned to see Mr. Black in the doorway.

Tom stood up from the table. Clara clapped her hands. But Martha was fastest. She overturned her chair, running to him.

"What's going on?" my grandmother asked.

"It's Mr. Black," Tom said.

"You're soaking," Martha said.

"He's getting footprints all over your floor," Clara said.

Martha fussed at him, tucking in his collar, checking his hands for scratches.

"If I'd known I would get this kind of reception," Mr. Black said, "I would have died again a long time ago."

I was the only one who didn't get up. Even my grandmother stood and smiled uncomfortably at nothing. But I didn't. I didn't even look at him. I lowered my head into the blanket that still wrapped me, and peered down at my teacup, its delicate handle and rose pattern. My grandmother had expensive, old china. I remembered being warned against breaking it—or even using it at all—when I was child.

I was warned against the balconies; warned against the barn, and the train, and the widow's walk, and the road, and the door to nowhere, and the myriad ways she thought I could get hurt or get in trouble around the house.

But my grandmother had never said anything, never warned me at all, about the ghosts.

"Esmé, I'm fine," Mr. Black said. He was right beside me, crouching down to my level. "Soaked but fine."

"I'm sorry," I whispered.

"I'll dry off soon enough. One of the ghost advantages."

"I'm sorry you had to save my life again."

He looked at me through half-closed lids. "If you still have a life, you might as well keep it."

Clara rolled her eyes. She toyed with her full cup of tea, in a way that seemed to indicate she was going to spill it soon. "I just don't see what the fuss is. She's alive—but she won't be forever. No one will. It doesn't make her special."

"No." Tom slipped his hand over mine. "It makes her capable."

And then, he put our hands under the table, on my lap, and turned his over so that I alone could see the underside. I could see his palm. Burned into the skin—how could I never have noticed it before?—was a scar, a brand: the mark of the Stationmaster's lantern, the sign of his hurt. *Dietz*.

I had a matching brand on my own palm, the letters new, red and raised.

"Yours will fade," he whispered.

"Maybe she's hiding," I said. "My sister is smart. She ran and she's hiding from him. She's waiting him out."

"We just have to find her before he does," my grandmother said.

Martha stayed in the room with me that night, and Clara with my grandmother, while Tom and Mr. Black kept looking for my sister. Martha tucked me in, then sat on the end of the bed. I lay on my back, wide awake, watching the ceiling.

On the ceiling of the apartment in New York, my sister and I had glued stars, little florescent stickers that glowed at night in a way real stars never did. Still, it was comforting to look up there and see—not darkness—but neon spots. I couldn't remember if I had been afraid of the dark as a child. I must have been. I couldn't remember when the dreams about my mother had started. They were not a comfort, but a sad reminder. And why did I never dream of my father?

Here, on the ceiling at my grandmother's house, there were no stars: only the ceiling, blank and white, flaking in parts. There were brown spots of water damage in the corners, too big for me to pretend they were stars.

I was never going to see the apartment in New York again, I realized, and just as quickly, I realized I wasn't sad about it.

"Is Mr. Black going to be okay?" I whispered in the dark.

"Fine," Martha said. "Ghosts are resilient."

"Why is it so bad, reliving your death? Does it hurt?"

Martha was silent a moment. Then she said, "Yes. And more than that, it brings back feelings."

"What kind of feelings?"

"The feelings you had when you died, what you were thinking, what you were worrying about. You forget that you're a ghost and nothing worse can happen to you than what already happened. You panic. You go through it all over again, everything you felt the first time."

"Is it lonely dying?"

"Yes," she said.

We watched the ceiling for a while. With anyone else, at a slumber party maybe, I would have thought the other person in the room with me would have fallen asleep. But the other person in the room was a ghost, and she could not sleep, so I spoke, after a long silence, without fear of waking her. "Mr. Black is pretty okay," I said. "He saved my life. Twice now, and the second time was really hard. I know he didn't want to do it."

"No," Martha said.

"But he did. He's really brave, once you get past the whining. And nice and funny, once you get past the booze. And he's loyal."

"Miss?"

"I don't know. I just think he's trustworthy, that's all. I think you could trust him. You know, with your heart."

The silence lasted longer. Outside the window, I heard a cat. I didn't hear Tom or Mr. Black, but I knew they were out there, walking in the darkness of the yard or woods, searching.

Finally Martha said. "Yes, Miss. I suspect Mr. Black is. Trustworthy."

And then I could sleep.

In the morning, my grandmother went to file a police report on my sister. Martha and Mr. Black went with her, even though Mr. Black said ghosts didn't like cars. But I pushed him in the direction of the station wagon: "You and Martha sit in the back. Together."

Martha shot me an alarmed look.

I watched the ghosts get into the backseat, Mr. Black holding the door open for Martha, my grandmother adjusting the rearview mirror and seeing nothing, I knew, but still pretending. They drove off, Mr. Black staring mournfully at me through the back window.

Tom and I kept researching, unearthing the last of my grandmother's books. I felt like I had to keep searching for answers. I had to keep my fingers turning pages, my eyes scanning words; otherwise, they would well up with tears and I would not be able to get them to stop. "One week," I muttered.

I hadn't realized I had spoken aloud until Tom said, "What's that?"

I looked up from the book I was paging through, something unhelpful on exorcisms. "Louise, the girl at school—she was missing for a week. That seems to be the pattern with the runaways. They were found after a week. Found dead."

Tom frowned. "But that could have been just when they were discovered. They could have died earlier."

"I know. But I don't think so. The Stationmaster lured them to very public places, the train tracks usually. I think he wanted them to be found right away, for people to know what he had done, for some reason. People go to the train station every day. They would have noticed if the ... the ..." I couldn't still say the word *dead*. Not when my sister was missing. "If the bodies were there earlier," I said. "Where did the Stationmaster take you?"

"Nowhere," Tom shrugged. "Our house."

But their house had burned down.

Clara had torched it, years ago. I asked him to take me there anyway, and we stood together in the empty field. From here, my grandmother's house looked like a thumb. I could see the silo, the barn in ruins, but much of the house was hidden by the hill. Only the top story and the widow's walk were truly visible. We sat down in the overgrown grass. The field was a blank, beige space. There were no hiding places.

My sister was not here.

"There's nothing," I said. "No foundation. No trace of your shack at all."

"No," Tom said. "Not even ashes."

"Does that make you sad?"

He shook his head. "It wasn't a happy place, Ez. I wouldn't want to remember it."

"But you lived here."

"To tell you the truth, I always felt like I lived at your grandmother's house," he said. "I could see it from my window at night, all lit up, and I used to dream about it, what it was like there, the fancy parties, the food they must have had, what it was like to grow up in that house—Clara and I used to talk about it, to imagine. We would pretend to be invited to dinner parties there, these elaborate feasts. Clara was very good at it, especially imagining the sweets."

I looked toward the house again. "From here, you could see the Builder fall."

"Yes."

I stood up. "The Builder," I said. "If anyone would know hiding places, he would."

Tom said just to follow the sound of hammering. It led us to the barn.

I had only been in the barn twice; once when Mr. Black had hid me from the Stationmaster in the hayloft, and again yesterday evening, looking for the Firecracker. I had searched in every corner, turned over moldy mounds of hay, finding nothing.

The barn looked different in daylight. We found the Builder on the first floor, and I saw why it seemed so sunny: light was streaming in through the sides of the barn. The Builder was prying boards off the wall with a hammer.

"What are you doing?" I asked. Sawdust sank beneath my feet as Tom and I approached him. The air stank of pigeons.

The Builder considered the board he had just wrenched from the side of the building. "Reclamation," he said. "I'm putting this old lumber to use. It will give the house character."

"Where are you going to put it?"

"I haven't decided yet. Perhaps another staircase?"

I tried not to breathe in the pigeon-scented air of the barn. I felt my patience dissolving. "Look," I said, "you might find you're a lot happier if you just go ahead and finish the thing."

He looked at me, startled. "Finish the house?"

I kept thinking of Martha running into the house, running into the kitchen, hiding her face. She had given up her life for this man, this man who was married, this man who didn't notice anything that couldn't be sanded, stained, or hammered. "The house is pretty good, already," I said. "Just go ahead. Call it a day. Move on."

"Ez," Tom said. "Remember why we're here."

"We have a question for you," I said flatly. "A question about the house."

"Oh?" the Builder said. "A beauty, isn't she?"

"Sure," I said.

"I believe I shall call her the Lower Vale. Vale is my Christian name, as you may know, and one might imagine the Higher Vale would be more appropriate, but Emily thinks that is presumptuous, and also, we already have established a Higher Vale of sorts, a family plot to occupy the field above the pond. A lovely place, shaded. Again, my dear wife believes that is putting the cart before the horse, but I think it's best to be prepared, to prepare ourselves, to have a comfortable place ready for us when we pass."

"You're buried in the family cemetery?" I asked.

He blinked at me, stroking his mustache. "I *will* be."

I felt Tom's hand on my arm: "He goes in and out of it. Knowing he's a ghost. Remembering."

The Builder was studying me. "I have a Chinese servant, you know," he said. "Lovely young woman. Good with the children. Hardworking. A bit superstitious."

171

"Right," I said quickly. I didn't care if he didn't remember he was dead. I didn't care if he had died a horrible, violent way. The Builder hurt Martha, and he talked too much, and he was starting to offend me. "We need to know where the hiding places are around the house," I said. "Right now."

"Hiding places?"

"Trick wall? Hidden staircase? Someone is missing."

"Good heavens," the Builder said. "You know, my wife Emily thought it unwise to move into the house before its completion, to allow the children to play there, but I think—"

"Now," I said. And when Tom looked at me, I said, "Please."

"There are the servant steps," the Builder said. He looked up at the loft as he recalled. "There's a loose board in the piano lid. My son hides his bug collection there. There's a tunnel under the house. It predates the house, from the war between the states, and people said when I bought this land, there might be ghosts in the tunnel. My Chinese servant says—"

"Thanks," I said. "You've been really helpful." Tom took my hand, and we started quickly toward the barn door, but I looked over my shoulder. "Think about finishing the house," I said to the Builder, who stood clutching his board. "It's pretty good the way it is now. Think about just letting it go."

"That's not going to do any good," Tom said when we were outside again.

"It's what he wants. He *wants* to finish the house. If he thinks it's done, if he decides it is, he can vanish, he can stop being a ghost. And then he can go on his way, and Martha can fall in love with Mr. Black."

Tom looked startled. "Martha and Mr. Black?"

"Seriously, Tom, where have you been for a hundred years? They're made for each other. Now, let's check the tunnel."

"Clara already checked the tunnel."

172

"I know," I said. "But she went in her entrance, right, through the kiln? The tunnel comes out into the kitchen. And when I ran into the Stationmaster after my sister disappeared, he was outside near the kitchen, like he had just been there." I remembered the pond, his hands on my hair ...

"Are you all right?" Tom asked.

I shook it off. "Fine."

My sister had been good about closing doors, keeping the cats out. But my sister wasn't here anymore, and in the kitchen, Manxes perched on the counter, a chorus of meows greeting us at the door.

I brushed the cats away, checking cabinets, behind the fridge. "Feel on the walls," I said, opening the pantry door.

Tom kneeled and pushed on the wall beside the stove. "What am I feeling for?"

"I don't know. Something that gives. Something that feels hollow."

Tom pushed harder. The wall didn't budge. I kneeled beside him and pushed so hard the force shot me backward, into the cabinet. A can of tomato sauce on the counter behind me fell and rolled onto the floor. It made a thud when it landed.

A hollow thud.

"What about a trapdoor?" I asked.

Tom was already beneath the kitchen table, pushing away the rag rug, and putting pressure on the boards.

I rolled the can away, and knelt beside him. "You've never come up this way before?"

"It's Clara's tunnel. She's the one who found it. She's the one who spends her time there. Clara likes secrets and passageways and tunnels. I don't like to be underground so much. It reminds me."

173

I thought of the dark place they had taken me that day: the kiln and the ladder made of bricks, the smell of earth and dust. Of course they had taken me there. Clara's idea, apparently. What better place to tell someone she's dead, to try and convince her, than underground?

"Tom," I said, "what happened to Clara? I thought she was my friend, and then …"

"She is your friend," he insisted. "She's your friend the best way she can be."

"Did something happen to her?"

"Yes," Tom said. "The Stationmaster happened to her."

"Here we go." I dug with my hands in a crack between the boards. It was a square.

A door.

"It's stuck," Tom said.

"Just locked. There's a latch." I traced my fingers down the sides of the door until I found it: rusted metal. I slid it to the side. There was a click.

It took a while for my eyes to adjust. I thought it would be less scary this time, being in the tunnel, in part because I knew the one standing beside me in the shadows now. I had his hand in mine. I also knew where the tunnel ended. I knew where it came out, even if I couldn't see the end yet.

But when we stood in the cool darkness, after Tom had pulled the trapdoor closed above us to prevent the cats from following, I felt a familiar panic. Yes, I had been here before. But that was before I had met the Stationmaster.

Slowly the pattern of the tunnel's walls revealed itself. I could see Tom's face beside me. "There's just no place to hide down here," he said. "There's no crevice. There are no other tunnels branching out. Just this one, long and straight. And it's empty." We were traveling the length of the tunnel, slowly scanning it. "Wait," he said. He stopped, and I crashed into him. He paused. "There's someone here."

"My sister!" I let go of his hand to reach into the shadows. I felt nothing, then my fingers grazed a shoulder. I grabbed it. "You're all right!" I said. "You're all right. Why aren't you saying anything?"

A strange voice answered. "Because I don't know who you are."

CHAPTER 16

A Nice Dare

I pulled my hand back.

"Who are you?" Tom said.

"I might ask the same of you," the voice said. It was thick and low.

I began to back up. I raised my arms to the roof of the tunnel, blindly searching for the trapdoor. Where was the door? Why had we closed the door?

"Why haven't I met you before?" Tom said.

"Been traveling," the voice said.

There was another sound then, and a tear-shaped spark lit the darkness. The spark flared and brightened, growing bigger, the light skipping over a hand as it bent to the ground and lit something.

A lantern.

But the light flickered, brightening the tunnel and the hand, the arm, the face of the figure who had struck the match. The woman. It was a woman, as old as my grandmother and round, wearing a long dress and a holey blue shawl. Her skin was lined. A ghost, I knew. I knew right away. I tried to calm down, to slow the thrum that beat through my chest. My heart was thudding, and I felt tightness in my arms and legs. I kept my voice steady. "Where did you come from?" I asked.

"Virginia," the ghost said.

I thought for a moment. "Virginia was a slave state."

"Yes," the ghost said. "And Pennsylvania is free."

The tunnel. The tunnel was a part of the Underground Railroad, used to hide slaves as they escaped to freedom.

"Well, you made it," I said, too brightly. "You're free. You can go now. You can stop being a ghost."

"Go?" the woman said.

"The war is over."

"She might want more than freedom," Tom said.

"Her *name* is Lucy," the ghost said.

"Hi Lucy," Tom said. "I'm Tom and this is Esmé."

"We don't have time for this," I whispered. "My sister ..."

He squeezed my hand. "What have you been doing all this time, Lucy?"

Lucy looked away from us, toward the darkness. Somewhere in the distance the tunnel ended in a ladder and a kiln, in a tree and a field, in sunlight. It seemed very far away. "Oh, I've been waiting for the others," she said.

"The others?"

"My sister and her children. They'll come soon, I expect. They were right behind me."

Even in the shadows, I could feel Tom looking at me.

"Maybe they got out," I said. "Maybe they're already free. There were ... *are* ... lots of stops on the Railroad between here and Virginia, right?"

"That's true," Lucy said. "And we've got this." She set her lantern down in order to hold something up, a big colorful sheet. A map, I thought, but bigger and brighter than any map I had ever seen.

I leaned closer and regarded it in the lantern light. I saw it was a blanket, a quilt. The colors were explosions in the darkness, blue and orange and green, half-lit by the flickering flame. I leaned closer and saw patterns, geometric shapes. I wanted to touch the quilt but stopped myself, my hand hovering over the squares. "It's beautiful."

"It gives hope," Lucy said. "And advice. Reminders mostly. See here," she pointed to a sunburst pattern. "That's the North Star. This one, that's the Drunkard's Path. That reminds you to change your way, vary it up, move east and west, zigzag like a drunk."

"Like Mr. Black," I said.

"Important to keep moving. Important to follow the star. That's what I told her." She folded the quilt away and as she did so, lifted the lantern to peer into my face. "You look like her."

"Your sister?" I asked, confused.

"No. The girl."

"What girl?" I said.

"She came this way. Running from the house. Needing to get away fast. I don't know why. She looked like she had seen a ghost."

"Maybe she had," Tom said.

"Which way did she go?" I asked.

"Well, she had trouble hearing me," Lucy said. "But she needed a place to hide, and she seemed to understand my hands all right, so I pointed her on toward the other tunnel."

"The other tunnel?" I said. "What other tunnel?"

"Why," Lucy said, "the one for the train."

"Tom?" I said.

178

"It's not far. I don't why I didn't think of it before."

"Wait," Lucy said. "Be safe now. Follow the star."

Tom was tugging on my arm, and we had to go. I had to find my sister. I wanted to go, but something held me in the tunnel: Lucy's upturned face in the lantern light. She hugged her own shoulders: expectant, hopeful. She was waiting, still. How long had she been waiting?

"Thank you," I said.

She smiled at me. "I just wanted to help someone else."

And then she was gone. Even her lantern vanished. Without her light, the tunnel turned dim again, but I could make out a lumpy shape on the ground. The quilt.

"Wait a minute," I said to Tom. I picked it up. I folded it under my arms, and we ran and ran, then climbed out the kiln's secret entrance. The sun was glaring, welcome and hot.

I ran with Tom. Together, we passed the barn, the house, the driveway. We weren't flying, not exactly, but then we were across the road. Then we had left the train station behind before I had even realized it. We were traveling farther than I had ever gone in Wellstone. Had my sister really run this far, even in panic, even with a ghost behind her?

As abruptly as we started, we stopped. Tom set me down in the grass. Railroad tracks stretched in front of me, long and rusted. We had followed them to a valley. On both sides of the tracks, big brick walls rose up, marking the entrance to a train tunnel. I turned to my left and saw it: the huge black hole of the tunnel, a gaping maw.

"The tunnel's not that long," Tom said. "It curves—that's why you can't see any light." He reached for my hand and helped me up.

Together, we approached the mouth. We picked our way over the tracks, our shoes crunching over gravel and old, crackling leaves. Near the entrance, the tunnel walls were covered in graffiti, scarred with colors. I thought, for the first time in a long time, about the day I had gone into the subway tunnel in New York, the day everything had changed.

Was my gift already coming then? Had it already found me? Was I already starting to see ghosts—and was I already starting to fade?

I had gone into that tunnel for a boy, a boy I barely knew, a boy who didn't return my calls, who didn't know I was invisible now, who didn't even know I was alive, who didn't—I realized—know anything about me.

And *he* wasn't alive.

The truth jolted me. No one ever spoke to Acid, no one ever talked about him but me; my old classmates looked at me like I was crazy when I did. His mother cried when I had tried to call. I was sent to the counselor who lectured me about my dream world; I was told about the dangers of lies.

It wasn't a dream world. It was a dead world.

There had been an accident, the subway worker who had pulled me out of the tunnel had said. A boy had died in this very tunnel. A boy had died. A boy. Telling me that he loved me— telling *someone* that he had been alive, that he had loved—was that what he needed, all he wanted? Was that what had caused him to go?

Walking on the railroad tracks, I knew I would never see that ghost again. I went into the tunnel with another boy. How long before he too would disappear?

I squeezed his hand and he smiled down at me.

"Nothing to worry about, Ez," he said, his voice reverberating.

We were inside the tunnel, the high sides rising up like a cathedral. We walked alongside the tracks, close to the wall—so close, brick brushed my shoulder. The walls curved around the bend. I looked back until the light from outside disappeared. We walked on in the darkness and cold.

"Kids come here a lot," Tom was saying.

"And do what?"

He shrugged.

I stepped over a flattened beer can. "Oh."

"There's not a lot to do in Wellstone," Tom said. "This place makes a nice dare."

"Coming here? It's not so bad." I looked up at the arched ceiling, far away.

"Coming here when the trains come through," Tom said. "That's the dare."

I dropped his hand. "Trains? Trains come through here? This track is active?"

There was a foot or two of space between the gravel path along the wall and the tracks. That was it. If a train came through, we would have to flatten ourselves against the wall to avoid being hit. Even then, I wasn't sure we would make it.

Why would my sister come here?

"Look." Tom beckoned me further along the track. He was running his hands over the wall, feeling for something. He turned back to smile at me, then he was gone; he was just gone.

"Tom!" I said. "Don't do that ghost thing."

"It's not a ghost thing." His voice was muffled. I heard a scratching, then his face appeared at knee level. I bent down. I saw a small brick alcove set into the bottom of the tunnel wall, barely big enough for one person to crouch inside, as Tom was doing.

"It's a recess," he said. "A bay set into the wall. For safety."

181

I studied it. "I hid in one of these. It was a little bigger, though. In New York. When I hit my head." It was not a pleasant memory, and I straightened quickly.

Tom crawled out of the recess, dusting himself off. "They're all over, every few feet on both sides of the tracks, these safety bays. In case a worker is trapped here when a train comes through, he can duck inside the bay and wait until the train passes. That's what kids do when the train comes. That's the dare: to wait out the train."

"How do you know this?" I asked.

"I was a kid once. A real one. That was a dare, even then. It's safe in the bay, but you have to wait out the train."

"Wait it out," I said blankly. "You think my sister is in one of these? You think that's where she's hiding? Can she hear us?"

"I don't know. It's an idea. I hid here a few times when … I needed to."

I kept my voice steady. "Did he know? Did the Stationmaster know about your hiding place? Did he ever find you here?"

"Yes, he did," Tom said.

I began to run, racing alongside the tracks, ducking to look in each of the safety bays as I passed. They were dark. They were all dark. I yelled my sister's name. I slipped on a patch of gravel and slid, reaching out to catch myself, touching the track as I fell. I thought it was the third rail, the live rail. I pulled my hand back quickly.

But it wasn't electricity that coursed through my bones. It was a sound, a deep rumbling bass.

Tom lifted me off the ground. "We have to get out of here. *You* have to get out of here."

"What's going on?"

"A train's coming."

Now I could feel it through my feet. The ground shook, and there was a roar, low and heavy. It vibrated in my chest. I heard a long blast.

"Come on!" Tom said.

"No!" I pulled back from him. "My sister. What if she's here?"

"If she's here, she's hiding. She'll be safe."

But I found my footing, and ran away from Tom, away from our exit, back into the heart of the tunnel, shouting for her. I dashed around the curve—and I could see the light then. The light was yellow and powerful. It looked familiar.

It was the headlight of a train.

"Esmé!" Tom shouted.

I stopped dead still. A shadow stood in the middle of the light, out on the tracks ahead of me. It was moving—no. Dancing. *She* was dancing, lifting her slender arms, making graceful dips and bows. The light was so bright, the figure black and featureless, only a silhouette, but I recognized the hair in its high dark bun, the long curve of the neck.

My sister.

"What are you doing?" I shouted at her.

"What are *you* doing?" Tom said.

I just stared at my sister. Something was different, something was wrong. It was her, but it was not her. The way she moved was off. She kept dancing, not seeing me, unfazed by me. I stood frozen, watching her, and watching the light behind her grow bigger, closer.

"Move out of the way!" Tom said. He wrapped his arms around my waist and pulled.

We fell together into the gravel beside the tracks. I was fighting with him, trying to twist out of his arms. But he was stronger. Even or especially as a ghost, he was stronger.

He dragged me to the wall, felt around blindly, then located the safety bay. He pushed me inside.

The train horn came again, so loud and close, I cried out. Plaster trickled from the walls. The safety bay was a tight space, barely big enough for me to crouch, my arms around my legs. I made myself into a ball. There was no door, just an archway for the opening, but Tom was not going to fit, I knew it.

I heard his voice, close to me. "Stay there!" he said.

I opened my eyes to see the entrance of the safety bay blocked by Tom. He had flattened himself against the wall, legs and arms spread. He was holding me in.

There was a blur of light and darkness and sound, a horn and a clanging and the growl of the motor, the groan of the tracks. The train passed. It took forever. Tom shook but did not move, shielding me. The tunnel seemed to shake too, trembling under the force of the train. Bits of the wall broke off and crumbled to the ground. I had dust in my hair and grit in my eyes. I squeezed them shut, and the sound of the train filled me—my lungs, my head, even my thoughts.

It was everything. It was death.

When it was over, the walls still shook, and the track hummed. No—it was my ears; my ears rang with the sound. I could breathe, I found, but I was choking, gasping, my throat and lips coated with a thick gray dust.

Tom unfroze. He reached into the safety bay and pulled me out, set me beside the tracks where I lay, coughing. He leaned over me.

I took a shuddering breath, and rolled over onto my side. I was eye level with grit and dust, the metal line of the tracks. "That's a dare?" I said. I pulled myself onto my knees. The tunnel was spinning. Tom put his arms out to me but I shook my head. I managed to rise. I was woozy, and my ears still rang, as though they were full of water. "That was how the Stationmaster died?"

"Something like that."

"Here? Was it here? Or somewhere else?"

"Here," Tom said. "How did you know?"

"I just know."

I took a stunned step. I looked around at the crumbling, graffitied walls. "This is an awful place," I said. "The safety bay isn't safe. It almost collapsed on me. The walls were falling in." I felt pain and looked down. There was blood on my ankle, and a shiny pink knot, already starting to swell.

"We'll take you to Martha," Tom said. "Martha will fix you up, tell you what to do."

I let him take my arm this time, and we hobbled together out of the tunnel. It was going to be a long trip back to the house, even if Tom carried me the whole way, even if he ran with me like the ghosts did. I wanted to sleep. When the sunlight hit my face, it was warm and sweet and hurt a little. I took a breath until my lungs rattled.

"Was that your sister?" Tom asked. "Did you see your sister back there, dancing in the light?"

"No," I said. I shut my eyes in the sun. "That was my mom."

CHAPTER 17

The Gift at the Table

By the time we reached the house, my grandmother had returned with Martha and Mr. Black.

"Can't even file a police report," my grandmother said. "Too soon for her even to be counted as missing. Not that they can *count* that high." Because the walls of the police station were full of posters, my grandmother said. Posters of missing children. Posters of runaways. Some of the posters were so old, they had turned yellow. Some were crumbling into bits. "I don't know why I didn't notice it before. So many children. But I never sensed that old man," my grandmother said. "I heard stories—but children are always afraid of the woods. People in small towns always talk, and many stories are made up."

"The Stationmaster isn't interested in you," I said, watching as Martha wound a long bolt of gauze around my ankle. My grandmother would have to help her, or the bandage wouldn't stay. The bandages on my hand kept dissolving every morning, even though the lantern burns beneath were healing. Tom was wrong; I would always have a scar.

"Still, I should have known," my grandmother said. She stood at the sink, shaking her head as she filled the kettle.

Tom and I had argued on the porch, before we went into the kitchen, argued about me seeing my mother's ghost, about me telling my grandmother about it.

"Your grandmother could help," he had said.

"It would only upset her."

"It's what she does. She talks to ghosts."

"*I* talk to ghosts. And see them."

"She has more experience than you."

"Not with seeing her own daughter's ghost she doesn't. Not with talking to her own dead daughter. She doesn't have experience with that. Besides, my mom didn't even say anything." I sighed. "Do you know what this means, seeing my mom in the tunnel like that today? It means the dreams I had of her weren't dreams. All these years, they weren't dreams. It was her ghost, trying to contact me, trying to tell me something. But she never *said* anything." My eyes filled with tears. "I never thought, when I was dreaming of my mother, to try and *talk* to her. I never knew to ask her anything. I never knew she was unhappy, that she wanted something. That she was a ghost." My eyes stung, and then the world was hot, spilling over.

Tom's arms went around me.

"Why is she a ghost?" I cried. "My dad isn't a ghost. They died together. Why isn't he a ghost with her? Why is she alone?"

"Did she die on a train?" Tom asked.

"No. A car. Someone ran a light and hit their car. It was raining." I swiped at my face with the back of my hand.

"Maybe she isn't alone," Tom said. "Clara and Martha and Mr. Black and me—we found each other. Maybe your mother found someone."

"Me," I said. I looked at him. My eyes were drying. "She found me. She reached out to me. But I don't understand what she wants."

We decided to stay in the ballroom that night, all of us. Not even the ghosts wanted to be alone.

My grandmother and I would sleep, and the ghosts would take turns hunting for the Firecracker and keeping watch: pacing the big square room, looking over us. It would be easier to watch us if we were in the same place, my grandmother said. Secretly, I thought she wanted to be able to keep tabs on me.

She found two musty sleeping bags and a couple of air mattresses Mr. Black tried to blow up. He cursed when the mattresses deflated after a only few minutes, huffing and turning purple, kicking a mouse's nest in the corner, until Martha gently took the mattresses from him, and I blew them up myself.

I hadn't been in the ballroom since I was a child. I hadn't remembered how high the ceilings were, how our voices bounced off the walls. The corners of the ballroom were strung with nests and cobwebs, the walls patchy with water damage. Still, it was lovely: wall moldings carved into arches, golden chandeliers only a little dark with burned-out bulbs. Every few feet, there was a mirror which made the room look even bigger, repeating itself a dozen times. Only a few of the mirrors were broken. The floors were hardwood, under the dust of years.

It reminded me, more than anything, of a dance studio.

I finished with the air mattresses, and unrolled the sleeping bags out in the center of the room. They were tattered with moth holes and smelled of mushrooms. I studied the patchy flannel lining, and became aware of Tom beside me. "We never did this in Girl Scouts," I said. "Not that I was ever in Girl Scouts."

"It's going to be okay, Ez," Tom said. "He can't get past the four of us. We don't need to sleep so we're the perfect guards."

"I won't be able to sleep," I said.

But I did sleep. Something about the slow, barely discernible click of footsteps on the perimeter, and the knowledge that those footsteps belonged to friends, looking out for me; something about the single chandelier we had left on, like a nightlight, how it was reflected in the mirrors a dozen times, a dozen nightlights; and something about how my grandmother slept close to me, so close I could reach out and grab her hand if I needed to—it was comforting. It was enough. I slept.

I woke up to shouting.

Then, the smell. Acrid and ashy, like fall leaves. No, like wood smoke. I shifted in the sleeping bag, not yet fully awake. Was there a campfire? I coughed, struggling to breathe in the dry air. It reminded me of when I had hid inside the chimney.

I bolted upright. My grandmother's sleeping bag beside me was empty. The ballroom looked dark. It was still night outside. I could see through the windows the deep black of well beyond midnight. And all the ghosts were gone, all except Mr. Black.

He leaned over me, jumping back when I sat up. "Stay there," he said.

"Where is everyone?"

"Stay *there*."

"What's that smell?"

He shook his head. "You're supposed to stay there. Your grandmother said. I'm supposed to watch you and keep you safe, keep you alive."

"Forget that," I said. I zipped down the sleeping bag. "Where's my grandmother? Where's Tom?"

Then I heard them: the low voice of Tom and my grandmother's higher register. Someone was shouting. Someone was screaming. It was coming from beneath us. Downstairs.

I threw off the sleeping bag. Mr. Black moaned.

"It's not your fault, Mr. Black. You're a very good watchdog. Now, come on."

I ran down the stairs, Mr. Black close behind. On the steps, the smell became choking. I gasped, my eyes stinging. Mr. Black was tugging on my arm, trying to get me to go back upstairs. I shook him off and pulled my T-shirt up over my mouth and nose. At the bottom of the stairs, I saw orange. The sitting room glowed, as if every light was turned on.

The room was on fire.

"No!" Mr. Black said, pulling me back.

"My grandmother's in there," I said. I had reached the doorway, but Mr. Black didn't need to restrain me.

Flames held me back. They leapt from the curtain rods, tearing at the walls. The fire was orange and black, and it seemed to hang on the wall like long strips of burning wallpaper. But it moved like water, reaching out, lapping. It moved fast. Already, as I watched, it was spreading, jumping from spot to spot.

At the edge of the room stood three figures with their backs to me: Martha, Tom, and my grandmother. They were yelling at the fire. Tom was motioning with his hands while Martha put her apron to her face and cried. My grandmother was just standing there while the room burned down before her.

I stepped forward and grabbed my grandmother's arm. She turned, her eyes searching, still not seeing me. "Grandma," I said. "It's Esmé. What do we do?"

But it was Tom who answered. "Clara's in there."

I stared into the room. Behind the couch with the crocheted back where my grandmother had lain and listened to my voice on the tape recorder, where she watched TV night after night with no sound, another figure stood, sobbing. The fire lit her white hair.

Clara.

"What's she doing?" I asked.

"He's in there too," my grandmother said. "He's in there with her. I heard him."

He?

I dropped my grandmother's arm. I could see nothing in the room beyond the flames and the burning furniture, the black windows and Clara. "Grandma," I said. "Do you have a fire extinguisher?"

"Kitchen," she said.

I looked at Mr. Black. He started running.

Tom was calling to Clara, coaxing her. "Come on, Clara. You don't have to do this. Not again."

There was a crash as a curtain rod fell to the floor, fire spreading up it like a ladder. As it fell, I saw the glimmer of fire on glass. A lantern.

"He's by the window," I said. "The Stationmaster."

My grandmother nodded once and walked into the room.

"Grandma, no! What are you doing? He's a ghost. Fire can't hurt him."

She shook her head. She might have been talking to herself. "This has gone on long enough," she said. She raised her voice, like she had in the house of Kate's ghost. "Spirit, leave this place."

"Grandma!"

She was approaching the window, her arms outstretched.

191

"You can't reason with him," I said. "You can't talk to him. Not him."

"Come on, Clara," Tom said.

My grandmother had reached the couch. A crash as the second curtain rod fell. Flames were spreading across the ceiling now, churning and boiling. Flames reached the couch and raced across the back of it. Clara's face looked orange and red.

"Clara, not again!" Tom said. "Don't do this to me again. Don't leave me."

"You left me first!" Clara said.

"Spirit!" my grandmother said.

A crash. But not another curtain rod: the window had been smashed. Someone had broken the window—and through it, the Stationmaster had escaped.

Cool air rushed into the room through the broken window. It seemed to give the fire strength. The flames on the ceiling poured across the whole of it now. The couch burst into fire with a scream, Clara's scream, and I heard sirens in the distance. I heard the footsteps of Mr. Black running behind me, returning with the fire extinguisher he probably wouldn't know how to work, and the work wouldn't last, and I saw my grandmother take a step back as a flame sped across the carpet and licked the hem of her nightgown.

I didn't think. Beside me, at the edge of the room, was the piano. And on top of the piano, folded where I had left it, was the quilt, the slave quilt the ghost Lucy had given me. I grabbed it and threw it over my grandmother, wrapping the sides around her in one quick motion. The fire had eaten the bottom of her nightgown. Pieces fell away like blackened paper. I held her in my arms, the quilt dampening the flames, and backed us out of the room.

*

We sat in the kitchen until the sun came up.

I made the tea. My grandmother, silent, sat in a chair at the table, and looked at her lap. Half of her nightgown had burned away. She smelled of smoke—the quilt did, her hair did, we all did.

Mr. Black had tried to put out the flames, but they seemed to dampen, all on their own, to just go out. The fire department came, and my grandmother had gone to the door, shuffling in her bare feet and quilt, to explain to them that she had fallen asleep with a candle, that everything was fine now. They told her candles were dangerous, and inspected the room, and went away again.

And everything was fine. No one had been hurt, and the room would return. I knew it would. The work of the dead did not last. In a few hours, the room would be restored. Even now, ash was disappearing from the walls and ceiling. Curtain rods were returning to the windows. The hole in the glass was healing itself, the couch stuffing itself back in. I knew it. And Clara would show up, stunned and ashamed, fine, or maybe—probably—just as crazy as ever.

I leaned against the kitchen counter and studied the people assembled around the table, the living and the dead. Mr. Black sat next to Martha. He had fire extinguisher foam in his hair. He put his hand on Martha's and she didn't pull it back.

The water started boiling, steam ticking inside the kettle. Then the whistle: high-pitched and keening. The sound transfixed me, and I stood for a moment, staring at the white plume.

I thought of my mother, my mother in the train tunnel. All these years, when I dreamed about her dancing, I had dreamed about her in a black space with a bright light behind her. A stage, I had thought. A spotlight. But it wasn't a spotlight at all. It was a train's headlight. It had always been a headlight. I had always been dreaming, always without realizing it, of my mother in front of a train.

My grandmother turned and spoke to my stomach. "Hot chocolate," she said blankly.

"What?"

"The girl will want hot chocolate."

I sighed. "Grandma, she can't taste it," I said, and felt pressure on my arm.

My grandmother was touching my arm. My grandmother had *found* my arm, and touched it, and then she whispered: "With ghosts, it's always the thought that counts."

I wrapped the handle of the kettle in a tea towel. "Fine."

My grandmother nodded and removed her hand. Then she said decisively: "We'll find him."

I was focused on the drinks, looking for a tin of hot chocolate in a cabinet above the stove. "What?"

"All this time, we've been waiting for him," my grandmother said. "I have been waiting. And that was wrong. He came into my house. He threatened my granddaughter."

I found the tin and set it down. "Grandma."

"He took my other granddaughter."

"Grandmother."

"No," she said. "No more waiting. I am tired of waiting and running and hiding from him. From a ghost! We fight him now."

"You can't fight him. I tried. You can't hurt him unless you're a train. That's how he died."

"We fight him on our terms," my grandmother insisted. "We command him to speak."

"How are we going to do that?" I asked.

"Simple," my grandmother said. "Summon him."

I collected items from the kitchen on my grandmother's instructions: two shallow bowls, the saltshaker, a loaf of white bread. Tom took cinnamon sticks from a tin in the cabinet, rummaging around the spice shelves, looking for sandalwood.

"I don't think this is going to work," I said.

He reached his arm into the cabinet. "You've seen your grand-mother at work. You've followed her. She's good, isn't she?"

I shrugged.

"She hears ghosts, right?"

"I hear better than she does."

"She hears enough," Tom said.

Silver tins and mason jars full of powders and leaves cluttered the cabinets of the kitchen. Green and brown bundles in various stages of drying clustered on the ceiling, lashed to all the beams—that was life with my grandmother. I had never known what the herbs were for, never known about the candles, never understood about the cats (though Martha swore the cats were just cats). I remembered bits and pieces of my life with my mother: how she had dressed in red shoes; how she would knock on the door of a room before entering it, every time, every door; how she never turned around when someone tapped her on the shoulder—never, even if it was me.

All these years I had thought these were her quirks, little things I missed about her, things that made her herself. But why did she do them? How had she been raised in this big haunted house with its tunnel, with its ghost work that undid itself in the night, with my grandmother? What would that do to you?

What was that doing to me?

*

My grandmother had removed the sleeping bags from the ballroom. Taking their place was a large round table over which she was smoothing a white tablecloth. She glanced quickly at us. No—at the floating items coming in through the door in our invisible arms. "On the table, please," she said curtly.

This was the woman I had seen at Frank and Cindy's house: brisk, commanding. Martha pushed chairs in while Mr. Black stood in a corner, looking at the table with suspicion. "I'm not going to do it," he said.

"You'll be fine," my grandmother said.

"It's not natural. Ghosts calling ghosts! It's disgusting. Abysmal."

My grandmother ignored him. "Tom, get water for us to fill the dish."

Tom took one of the bowls away.

"Esmé, fill the other dish with salt."

I untwisted the lid on the saltshaker. Absentmindedly, I had been counting the chairs. The table was one short. "Grandma, you're missing a chair," I said.

She had pulled out the white candles from her big black bag. Now she was taking out a long kitchen match. She seemed not to hear me.

"Grandma?" I repeated. "There are five chairs. And six of us. Tom, Martha, Mr. Black, Clara, you and me."

My grandmother placed three candles at opposite points of the table, and bent to light them. I felt a shiver when I saw the flame from the match, remembering how the curtain rods had fallen, how the fire had torn across the ceiling. But my grandmother's face showed nothing. If she was still impacted by Clara's fire, she didn't show it. And she had heard me. "You are not sitting in," she said.

"What?" My hand jerked, knocking the shaker over. Salt spilled across the table.

"See?" she said. "You're careless. Not ready. Not the right person to have here."

"Grandma, that's not true. And I'll clean it up." I dumped the salt back into the shaker. "See?"

"Throw some over your shoulder," she said. "Please."

I did. "Grandma."

"No. You are not sitting in."

"Why?"

"I told you why. Besides, you're too young. Children should not be a part of this. Children are too susceptible. It's not safe."

"I've faced ghosts," I said. "I've faced *this* ghost."

"You have the gift," Clara said.

She had appeared in the center of the ballroom.

She was the same. Not a single yellow hair on her head looked singed. Not a ribbon was blackened. Her dress looked clean and bright; her curls, perfect. She was smiling the same strange grin. "That's what they say, anyway," Clara said. "You have the gift like your grandmother. Maybe better than your grandmother."

My grandmother's face showed no expression. She didn't look at Clara. I wondered if she had heard her. She finished lighting the candles, and blew out the match.

"Are you all right?" I asked Clara.

"Fine." Her face changed a little. "Embarrassed."

"You don't have anything to be embarrassed about. Oh, and I made you hot chocolate. It's downstairs."

"I'm sure it's cold."

197

"We can make more."

Her voice softened. "You can't sit in, Esmé, because there can't be two people with the gift at the table."

I turned to my grandmother. "Is that true?"

"Yes," she admitted. So she *had* heard. "It muddles things up. It could interfere."

"Why?"

"I don't know. But if you want this to work, I need you away from the table. You can watch us from the door."

I looked at the doorway where Clara was now twirling absently. Nothing had changed about her, apparently. "Why the door?" I asked.

"So if something goes wrong, you can run."

CHAPTER 18

Red Shoes

My grandmother began with a prayer.

It was the same prayer she had recited in the kitchen with Frank and Cindy, the prayer to St. Michael, a prayer of protection. My grandmother said she believed in a place after death, and she believed—she knew—that some people got stuck in the middle, got trapped in the layers: not quite living, not quite dead.

"That makes it sound as if we're in a cake," Mr. Black said.

There were many layers, my grandmother thought, many planes, and she had been afraid, when she could not find me at the train station that first day, that my gift had backfired and sent me to one of these shadowy levels, stuck among ghosts.

Or worse.

My grandmother held hands around the table with the ghosts. She asked them to close their eyes. From my position in the doorway, standing, with my arms crossed, I left my eyes open. I saw Mr. Black peeking at Martha beside him. I saw Clara open her eyes to cross them and stick out her tongue at my grandmother. I saw that only Tom and my grandmother were concentrating, eyes closed.

In the center of the table, my grandmother had arranged the bowl of salt, the bowl of water, now with a white feather floating in it, and the loaf of bread. After saying the prayer, she opened her eyes and pulled back her hands, motioning for Tom and Clara to join hands, completing the circle without her. My grandmother took a pinch of salt and sprinkled it in the water. Then, rising, she took the bowl and stepped a few feet away from the table.

I watched my grandmother kneel. She swept her wet fingers over the floor, tracing a circle with salty water. The floor was so dusty, you could see it, instantly. She crept around the table, ringing it.

"Spirit," she said, her voice booming. "I summon you. Show yourself to us in this place. Move among us and communicate with us." When the circle was complete, my grandmother stood and wiped her hands on her skirt. "No harm can come to us inside the circle," she said in her normal, quieter voice. "The circle will protect us."

I shifted in the doorway. I wasn't *in* the circle.

What did that mean for my safety?

My grandmother seated herself again at the table, re-joining hands with Clara and Tom. "Close your eyes," she said. "Clara, no peeking." Her voice changed again, became sonorous, official. I thought if I were a ghost, I would listen. "Spirit of the air, spirit of the ground, spirit of the house: show yourself to us in this place. Move among us and communicate with us. This bread is an offering to you."

This bread? She was offering bread to the Stationmaster? Plain white grocery store bread? I bit my lip hard to keep from saying something. The Stationmaster didn't want bread.

He wanted blood. Preferably mine, I thought. Or someone else young.

Not the Firecracker. Not her. Don't even think of that.

I tried to push the thought out of my mind, and then it was all I could think about. Had he hurt her, hit her with the lantern, burned her, pushed her down in the pond? Where was she? And was this really going to bring him? Would he tell us where she was; could we make him? I tried to focus on the table, where everyone sat, eyes closed, holding hands.

Nothing was happening.

"Clara, no peeking," my grandmother said.

"How can she tell?" Clara whispered.

"No, whispering, either." She raised her voice. "Spirit, I summon you. Show yourself to us in this place. Move among us and communicate with us."

Over and over my grandmother said this until I grew less and less afraid, more and more bored—and more convinced that the Stationmaster wasn't going to show. No one was going to show. My back ached and my legs were starting to tire. I sat down cross-legged, and slumped against the wall. I closed my eyes, just for a second.

The last thing I heard was the drone of my grandmother's voice.

I dreamed about the house. I was inside the house, my grandmother's house, but it was so much nicer than my grandmother kept it. The hardwood floors were gleaming, swept free of dust, reflecting the glow from the sparkling chandeliers. The wallpaper looked new—no water spots—and there were garlands hung across the moldings and draped over the mantles: thick dark greenery braided with bright white flowers. Everything was lit by candles, the flames sparking in men's glasses and ladies' earrings and shivery dresses.

Because the house was full of people. *Crazy dream*, I thought, sliding through the crowd. Everyone was dressed up: flowers and lace and jewels in their hair. Everyone was laughing. Waiters weaved through the halls, carrying trays of tiny pies and drinks in tall glasses and candies. I tried to reach for a treat, but the tray swept away from me, as if the waiter hadn't seen me.

I looked into her face. She wore a long black dress, a white cap. There was some kind of flower tucked behind her ear, small and yellow.

It was Martha.

"Martha!" I said. "Martha, it's me."

But my dream voice was muted, distorted and almost soundless, like I was speaking underwater. I could barely hear myself. And Martha couldn't hear me.

She disappeared into the crowd. I tried to follow, but the hallway was jammed, people in the dining room, people on the stairs, and I soon lost sight of her.

The crowd made way for a child, running through and laughing. She had big curls like Clara, but her hair was dark, and she was only five or six, dressed like a princess. Right behind her, chasing her, was a boy. I heard a muted shout. A woman followed the boy, a woman I had never seen before, with dark hair like the girl and a fancy white dress that shimmered in the candlelight. She scolded the children. At least, I think she did. The sound was distorted to me, faint and wavering, like my own voice had sounded in my ears.

I couldn't hear in my dream.

I left the woman and her children, and passed on through the crowd. I knew I was underdressed, in my usual T-shirt and jeans, but no one looked at me. No one seemed to see me.

I was invisible then, too.

I heard a deep belly laugh, dampened and warped so it sounded almost evil, and turned to see a mustache, a pocket watch, a stomach. It was the Builder. He was beaming, surrounded by friends who all laughed at his joke, whatever it had been, and downed drinks. I crept forward to the group and strained to hear them.

"Didn't think I could do it," he seemed to be saying. "And I didn't quite."

More laughter. I didn't understand what was so funny.

"Only the widow's walk left, in case Emily becomes a widow!"

Rollicking laughter this time from everyone. The dark-haired woman, the one who had scolded the children, glared at him, then moved quietly away.

"Would you like to see it?" the Builder asked his friends. "See the widow's walk, up on the roof?"

"No!" I said.

But of course no one heard me. They all made sounds of approval and moved toward the staircase, one glittering jovial mass.

"No!" I said again. "Don't go up there. You're going to *die* up there."

But the Builder led the group up the stairs.

So he had an audience, then, when he died.

Was this the first time? His original death? The night it had happened? I looked around at the party-goers, their champagne, their fancy dress. Was this New Year's Eve? Why was I dreaming this? Could I stop it? I tried to force my way through the press of people, to follow the Builder.

Then I saw a pair of red shoes.

I stopped. The shoes were attached to a small woman in a pale green dress with a ribbon on the back. She wore her hair in a black bun, like my mother always did. She was facing away from me, and she was moving fast.

I followed her. I fought my way through the crowd, pushing past people, stepping on toes. No one seemed to notice me. I followed the red of the woman's shoes, blood-red shoes.

My mother wouldn't tell me why she always wore red.

It had to be my mother I was seeing. It had to be. I followed her through the hallway, past the sitting room. In a corner near the door, under a neglected bunch of mistletoe, a man in black drank from a bottle, looking miserable.

The woman with the red shoes turned to go up the servant steps, surprising the servants who were streaming down the stairs with trays. I turned to follow her, and thought I saw in the corner of my eye, through the sitting-room window, a child's face, looking in from outside, a boy with black hair and bright-blue eyes, shivering in the cold as he watched the lovely party.

I didn't slow down. The woman was on the second floor now, and I tripped to keep up with her. "Mom," I said. "Mom, is that you?"

She didn't flinch, didn't stop, didn't give any indication that she had heard me. I still couldn't see her face as she turned and glided down the hall—only her red shoes, her green dress, and her gleaming black bun. She walked purposefully through the second floor and headed for the stairs to the third.

The crowd was thinner here: only a couple kissing in a corner hung with flowers. More mistletoe, I guessed, left over from Christmas; that was the flower Martha wore behind her ear.

I followed my mother up the stairs. "Mom," I kept saying. "Mom."

But she gave no sign that she had heard me.

On the third floor, I heard music.

And it was as if my ears had popped on a plane, like the bubble that had been surrounding me, muting and distorting everything in my dream, every sound, every word, burst. I heard the music sharp and clear.

A band stood on a little raised platform at the end of the ballroom, a quartet of musicians. In front of them, packing the floor, people danced—so many people, all dressed in jewels and tuxedos and dresses that glittered under the chandeliers. The room itself sparkled, reflected in the mirrors.

My head swam. It hurt my eyes, all those lights. I followed the red shoes as they slipped into the crowd, not dancing, but moving swiftly, instinctively through small gaps in the dancers: ducking under a raised arm, sliding between a talking couple. She seemed to anticipate how people would move, where there was going to be an opening for her to slip through while behind her, I crashed and banged into people, not watching where I was going, unable to predict who would move and who would stay still.

And just as my hearing had returned, it seemed my physical body had also. People felt it when I ran into them. They seemed to see. They stopped and glared at me, or said something rude to my back. I trod over toes, over a lady's hem. I heard it rip.

The woman with red shoes slid between a group in front of me, and was gone.

"Mom," I said. "Wait for me."

The music stopped. Before me, the crowd parted. And there was my mother.

She stood in the center of the ballroom. The crowd had moved back, surrounding her in a semi-circle as though she was going to start dancing a solo for them. She was more beautiful than I remembered. I hadn't remembered how much she looked like my sister, how much she looked like me.

She was smiling, smiling at me. She saw me; she actually saw me.

I felt my eyes clouding over and spill. I was weeping, trying to get the words out.

"Mom," I said. "Mom, I miss you. I don't know what to do."

She brought her finger to her lips. "Shh."

"I'm invisible. I don't know why. And I can see ghosts. Why can I see ghosts? Why didn't you tell me?"

"There wasn't time," my mother said. "I didn't know I wasn't going to have time."

"I know," I sobbed. My nose was running, my voice sticky. "Where's Dad? Is he okay?"

"Yes. I promise."

"What's going on? What's happening to me?"

"Shh," she said. "Remember the mail."

I sniffed. "What?"

"Remember the mail."

"What do you mean? What are you saying?"

"The mail, Esmé. When the time comes, and it will, remember the mail."

I felt panic. The crowd was starting to move again. The music was picking back up, and couples danced in front of my mother, filling in the circle. She was starting to disappear.

"Mom," I said. I couldn't see her through the crowd. I pushed at couples, trying to move them, but they ignored me, dividing us, keeping her from me. "Mom!"

I heard only her voice: "Remember to put out the mail."

"Mom, what do you want?" I cried.

Then there were hands on me, shaking me gently. One hand smoothed back my hair, another cradled my head. I lay on the floor of the ballroom. Faces peered over me: my grandmother, Martha, Tom. I slid up.

"Easy," Tom said.

"I'm okay. I had a dream."

"You fell on the floor and hit your head with a huge bang," Clara said. "Do you have a lump? Can I touch it?"

I felt the back of my head, brushing away Tom's and Martha's hands. "No. No, I don't have a lump and no, you couldn't touch it if I did."

"You were crying like a baby," Clara said.

I moved my hands from my head to my face. It was sticky and wet. Tears dampened the neckline of my shirt.

"Clara," Martha said.

"Screaming your head off, disrupting the circle."

"That's enough," Tom said.

I wiped at my face, and tried to smooth my shirt. "Did it work?" I asked.

Martha peered at me. "Did what work?"

"Did the séance work? Did the ghost come?"

"No," Clara said. "Nothing happened. It was the most boring thing in the world. More boring even than being dead."

"I came," a voice said. "I thought you all were calling me. I ... thought I heard my name. I hope I didn't interfere with anything."

I turned my head to see the Builder, standing with his hands in his pockets.

Then it came back, the dream. It all came back to me: the New Year's Eve party, the Builder, Martha. My mother. I looked at my grandmother. She looked like my mother too—all of us did—but tired. So tired.

I couldn't tell her. I knew I couldn't. I watched her try to find me, find my face, her eyes pouring over the floor, the space where I might be. Her face changed as she tried to look at me, crumpling like a tissue. She knew, somehow she knew, something was wrong.

"What is it, Grandma?" I asked.

"You act like you've seen a ghost," she said.

CHAPTER 19

It's Easy to Dye

The spirit had come at the séance. It had come to me.

She had.

I wrapped the blanket Martha had brought me tighter around my shoulders. It was Lucy's quilt, and it still smelled a little smoky, but I had asked for it. I had wanted something comforting, something at least a little familiar. I needed to think. *The mail, the mail.* My mother had said to remember the mail.

But I hadn't gotten any mail, not since I came to my grandmother's house. No one wrote letters. Not to me, anyway.

"Mr. Vale," I said, addressing the Builder. "You know this house pretty well, right?"

He stiffened. "I should hope so. I'm building her."

"Do you know if the mailbox was always where it is now?"

"The mailbox?" he repeated.

Behind his shoulder, I saw my grandmother freeze with her hand on the saltshaker. She was busying herself, putting away the items from the séance.

"Yes," I said. "Was it ever different? In a different place maybe?"

My grandmother was striding across the ballroom, clutching the saltshaker. "What's this about the mail?" she asked.

"I don't know," I said. "I was just wondering."

My grandmother dropped the salt. She didn't even bother to throw some over her shoulder. "What was it?" she said. "What was the vision? I know you had one. Who did you see?"

"You saw a ghost? The Stationmaster?" Tom asked.

"No," Clara said. "She'd be crying. Harder."

"What did they say?" Martha said.

I swallowed. I said it, *"Remember the mail."*

Everyone's face went blank.

"There was a mail slot," the Builder said, thinking. "In the front door. We didn't always have a mailbox—modern invention, bothersome, hooligans always smashing it down. The mail was delivered through a slot in the door. It's still there, if you want to see it."

"I do," I said.

But the mail slot wasn't there when the Builder, Mr. Black, and I went to check. The doors were solid oak.

"Oh dear," the Builder said, checking the doors from front to back. "It looks like these have been replaced. Did I do that? I don't remember doing that." Then he was lost in thoughts about the house. "We had a fantail light above the door," he said. "Stained glass. Expensive. Imported from France. We had a screen. My wife didn't like that. We made the roof conical, the porch wrap-around. Crown detailing for the roof peaks, radiating spindle details for the gables."

Now the Builder was just talking. Now he had forgotten me and Mr. Black. Now he would never say anything useful at all.

"The embedded corner tower ..." he said.

"Wait," I said. "There's a tower?"

"Why, yes. Finished it a few days ago."

"But it didn't last? The work of the dead doesn't last."

"Strangely, no," the Builder said. "So I built it again."

The tower was off the third floor, and it took us a while to get there because the Builder kept stopping to examine a step or fiddle with a balustrade, pulling a ball-peen hammer from his pocket and pausing to pound in nails. At the end of the hallway, past the ballroom, he slowed to push in a loose molding, and Mr. Black cried, "Oh, come on."

"Mr. Vale, where exactly are we going?" I asked.

He looked up at me, surprised, pulling on his mustache. He had forgotten about the tower, forgotten about the mail, forgotten about me, forgotten he was a ghost even, probably. But he said, "We're here."

Mr. Black sighed. "Here is a dead end. A hallway."

"I'm surprised you don't know it," the Builder said to me.

"Me?"

"My servant knows it."

I felt my chest get tight. I couldn't get angry; there wasn't time. I made myself say evenly, "I'm not your servant."

"No," the Builder said simply. "But she's your great-grandmother."

What did I know about the house, how it had come into my family? My mother had grown up here. So had my grandmother, and her mother had worked as a maid for the family of the house, the rich family who didn't want to live in their house because … because …

Because their father had died here.

The Builder rapped on the wall with his fist, and it popped open, a paneling of false wall creaking ajar.

211

I peeked inside and saw a staircase. "Where does that go?"

"To the tower," he said.

"Esmé, wait," Mr. Black said.

But I was already climbing into the passageway.

The walls of the secret staircase pressed in on me, a tight fit, with only enough space for me to crawl. I couldn't stand upright, or raise my head. And as I pitched forward, the steps behind me dissolved. My foot missed a step, and it slipped down onto nothing, into space. I kicked at the air.

The stairs behind me were gone.

"What's happening?" I said.

The steps below me were falling away like cards—and the walls on either side of the staircase started falling down too, melting. A plank was torn away, then another and another. It was like someone had thrown acid on the staircase. It was dissolving. I could see patches of the outside breaking through: the tops of trees, the purple sky, a star.

The work of the dead was undoing itself.

The Builder's tower was falling down.

My fingers scrabbled at the stairs. In my rush, I hit my chin on a step and slid down on my stomach, my legs kicking at the emptiness below. I swung and my arm touched a higher step. I pulled myself up.

There was nothing but air below me, waiting to swallow me. Above me, the staircase turned around a corner. I couldn't see where the bend led, but I vaulted up two more steps. I was at the top now, clutching the very last step. The staircase had ended, but there was no door at the top—just a solid wall. I couldn't climb any higher; there was nowhere to go. The staircase was going to dissolve and drop me.

I screamed.

Below me in the hallway, somewhere far away, the Builder shouted, "Push on the wall! There's a door hidden at the top, a secret door. Push on the wall."

The step beneath me, the last step, broke. But the wall at the top of the stairs had broken too. The trick wall collapsed beneath my shoulder, and I fell into the tower room with a scream.

Not my scream.

I was in the Builder's tower. But I was not alone.

I had fallen on my hands and knees. I could see tall black shoes. Shaking, I raised my head. The shoes were attached to black-clad legs. I saw arms, trembling a little. A pale, set mouth.

My sister.

I spoke her name.

"Esmé?" she said. Then her arms were around me, suffocating me, hitting my face and neck until she could find me—because she still couldn't *see* me—hugging me.

"Is it really you?" I asked.

"Is it really *you*?" she said, squeezing tighter.

I felt my limbs relax, felt myself fall into the hug. How long had it been since my sister had hugged me? I stayed in the hug for an instant longer than I ever would have in the past, then I glanced around.

The room looked small and very pink. There was a table with a pitcher of water, a daybed with rumpled blankets. One window was edged with colorful stained-glass squares. I had never seen the stained-glass window from the road, never seen this room at all.

"Have you been living here?" I asked my sister.

"Yes," she said.

"We've been looking for you. We thought you were in trouble."

"There was a man. He came in the house. He had a lantern. He was a ghost, wasn't he?"

I nodded grimly.

"I could see the lantern. I saw it swing out of the air, but I couldn't see him, so I knew what he was. I ran into the kitchen. My foot kicked the rug away by accident, and I found this door…"

"The tunnel," I said.

"Yes. I got outside from the tunnel, but then I got scared. I thought the man was in the tunnel, coming after me. I went back toward the house and then I saw a hammer and I met this other man, this … other ghost."

"The Builder," I said.

"He was nice. He built this for me." She gestured at the pink walls, the daybed, the pillows crimped in lace. "He misses his daughter, I guess. Anyway, he built it for me to hide in, to hide from the ghost."

"But the work of the dead doesn't last," I said.

"No. So when the room collapsed, he built it again. And again."

"He's been building you rooms and shutting you up in them?"

"Something like that. And he covered my tracks, went back and locked the trapdoor in the kitchen, he said. The other man didn't come. The ghost with the lantern didn't come back. He can't find me, I guess."

"Nobody could."

"Who's the ghost with the lantern, Esmé? What does he want?"

I didn't answer. I was glancing around the room. There were pictures taped to the pink walls, old images cut from magazines and vintage newspaper ads. I saw a picture of a girl in a white dress and parasol. *Pears Soap* it read above her head. Another ad featured girls in blue dresses dancing with the ribbons of a May Pole. *It's Easy to Dye with Peterson's Dye*, the ad read. The girls were all smiling.

"Listen," I said to my sister. "Did the Builder ever say anything about the mail?"

"No. What do you mean?"

"The mail? Putting out the mail, or where the mail goes?"

Her eyes narrowed. "Why? What's going on, Esmé?"

We heard a crack, the sound of a board splitting. We both looked down to see a zigzag shape in the floor, a lightning-shaped rend, getting wider.

"When the room falls apart," I said quickly, "what happens?"

"I don't know. I'm gone by then. He moves me to another hiding place."

"And you never found me or Grandma? You never told us you were okay?"

"I didn't know where I *was*, Esmé. I didn't even know if I was in the house still. My phone is dead. I didn't know if I was okay. I saw lanterns and floating hammers and saws."

Another crack. This one shook the room, and we stumbled, knocked to our knees.

"We have to get out of here," I said.

"How?" My sister pointed to the wall.

There was the hole through which I had burst, a me-sized hole in the false paneling. But behind it, there was only air, empty space. No stairs anymore. The stairs had all broken and faded away. With a ripping sound, shingles began to fall from the roof above us.

"It's breaking apart!" I said. "The room is collapsing."

"Why does it do this?"

215

"Because the dead made it."

The roof dissolved with a roaring sound. The sky was the roof now, open to the dark and windy night. We got down on our hands and knees. With a groan, the floor collapsed. The Firecracker screamed, and we sank, only to land on the roof, slanted and prickly with shingles. We clutched at them. The walls were disappearing above us. I raised my head, wincing at the wind, and watched the table in the room collapse like a cake. I watched the daybed vanish.

"The mail," I said. "The thing about the mail—a spirit said it to me." I moved my hand for a better hold. How much of the roof was built when the Builder was alive, and how much of it had he done when he was dead? Would his living work still last? I tried not to look down. "She said to remember the mail," I said. "She said to remember to put out the mail."

"She?" the Firecracker said.

I watched the pink walls get lower and lower. I watched the dye ad roll up and vanish. My arms were getting tired of holding on, my hands scratched from the climb up the stairs. I tried to look around, to spy a way off the roof, and almost lost my grip. "Grandma had a séance," I said.

"*What?*"

"We were trying to find you, to call the ghost who was hunting you. If you had just come downstairs—"

The Firecracker said, "This is why I was nervous about you coming here. Grandma thinks these things are no big deal. She thinks you can just play with ghosts."

"Why didn't you warn me? Why didn't you or Mom say anything?"

Now there were only two walls above us. Now my fingers had begun to shake.

"I thought there was something wrong with me," the Firecracker said, adjusting her hold on the roof. "Mom never said it would happen. I thought I was going crazy. And I thought I could make it stop."

"How?" I asked.

Now one wall was left of the tower room. Now the moon came out from behind a cloud, bone-white and full, casting the roof in silver.

"I stopped dancing," the Firecracker said.

In spite of everything, I laughed.

The Firecracker turned her head to look at me, where she thought I was; she was almost right. "I saw Mom. That's why I stopped. Because I saw Mom at a performance. My last show, the one *The New York Times* wrote up? She was there."

I lost my grip and slid down the roof.

The Firecracker cried out, but she couldn't save me; she couldn't *see* me. Shingles snagged at my stomach. My feet fell over the edge of the roof. I kicked and felt air. I had nothing to hang onto, nothing to hold.

My legs fell over the roof. My stomach, my chest, my shoulders slipped. My chin hit the rain gutter. I clutched at it with one hand but with a groaning sound, the gutter ripped away from the roof. I dropped it. I saw a flash of the ground as it fell, the spot that awaited me. My feet kicked out.

And this time, they connected with something solid. I grasped the edge of the roof with both hands, and with my shoe found the solid footing. I wrapped my leg around it.

A ladder.

CHAPTER 20

Dearest Annabelle

I stood on the ground, peering up in wonder. The roof of the house appeared flat, and the walls of the secret room were gone. There was no sign at all of the tower that had sheltered my sister. "We've got to figure this mail thing out," I muttered.

The Firecracker looked up unsteadily. "Esmé, there's one ghost out there who's trying to kill us. Why does it matter what another one said?"

"Because it's important."

"Why?"

"Because I trust her," I said.

And then she knew. She knew without me telling her. My sister knew. I had seen our mother. I had talked with her.

The Firecracker stared into space for a second, and then she took her phone out of her pocket. Her movement had a slow purposefulness that frightened me. "I'm going to get this thing working," she said. "The battery is dead. I'm going to get reception, somehow, even though it barely works here, and I'm going to call a cab—we are *not* taking a train—and then I'm going to get us the hell out of here, back to New York."

"We don't have a place in New York anymore. We don't have anywhere else to go."

"I'll find somewhere to go. Just not here. We have to get out of here. Tonight."

"Here is home." As soon as I said it, I knew it was true. "Grandma lives here. Mom grew up here. Tom and Clara and Mr. Black and Martha and the Builder are here. They need us. Here."

"They're dead, Esmé," my sister said. "They don't need us."

I became aware that Tom and the others had gathered and were behind us, watching. "They do," I said. "They're still here because they need something, and we can give it to them. We can help them. We can hear them. We're the only ones."

"I can't help them," my sister said.

"Yes, you can. We all can. And the living need us here too."

"*What* living?" my sister said. "Grandma's the only other real live person I've seen since I've been here."

I told her about the runaways.

When I was finished, she crossed her arms. "There's either a lot of unhappy kids out there who just left home, which is totally possible, or a real killer—and you want to chase after a *ghost*?"

"He came for you," I said. "What do you think about him?"

She was silent, looking at her phone. "What do you want to do?"

"Listen to Mom," I said. "Put out the mail."

"Well, it's night so the mail's not going."

Tom spoke up. "It is on the ghost train." The trains delivered mail during his time, he said, all of them carrying

219

letters from one town to the next. "Every station sent some out. Our train carried mail."

"Maybe Mom wrote you a letter," the Firecracker said. "Maybe she wants you to find the mail so you can read what she wrote."

I shook my head. "No. She said she wanted me to *put out* the mail—like, send a letter. Not pick one up."

"That doesn't make any sense."

"Little of what your mother did made any sense." My grandmother stood on the hill. "Studying dance," she said, walking toward us. "Going halfway around the world to do it, to France. Living there. Marrying a man I had never met, a non-Chinese man. Naming her daughters French names. Esmé and Collette. What kind of names are those? Turning her back on her family. Turning her back on her gift. When were you going to tell me you had seen your mother, Esmé?"

I spoke quietly, "It doesn't make sense, what she said."

"It never does," my grandmother said. Her mouth tightened. "But you still need to do it."

"Okay," I said. "So, if we all take shifts, we can—"

"No," my grandmother said. "*You* need to do it. She came to you. She spoke to you. Do you know how many times I looked for your mother? How many times I called to her? I wanted to ask her what to do for you two. I wanted to ask if she felt pain. I wanted to see her face, to tell her that I missed her, I missed her. But she never came to me. Not once."

"She came to the Firecracker."

"For like a second," my sister said. "And she never said anything."

"She came to you, Esmé," my grandmother repeated. "She spoke to you. She trusts you to do what she asked of you, to complete it."

"To send mail?" I said numbly. "What mail?"

Tom put his hand on my arm. "Let's start at the station, start with the trains."

So it was Tom who went with me. And Clara. And Mr. Black, Martha stepping up on tiptoe to peck him quickly on the cheek. "Be careful," she whispered.

And all through our silent trek down the hill, the ghost of a blush, an almost color, burned high on his face where she had kissed him.

When we reached the station, I stood on the platform, peering into the waiting area inside. It was dark and empty behind padlocked doors. The Stationmaster was not there. I knew that. I felt that, and yet I found myself straining to listen, dreading and, at the same time, waiting for his whistle.

I had only looked away for a moment, but when I turned back to the platform, Tom and Mr. Black were gone. I saw Clara at the edge and called to her. She looked at me deliberately, then hopped off the platform onto the tracks. I ran to the edge and looked down.

Clara had joined Tom and Mr. Black on the ground. They made a line, shoulder to shoulder. They stood right on the tracks, facing the way the train would come.

"What are you doing?" I asked.

"Stopping the train," Clara said.

"What? The ghost train won't stop?"

"Not if you want it to," Mr. Black said mournfully.

"Depends on the whims of the ghost conductor or whichever ghost is driving, if anyone is, and they're awfully unpredictable," Clara said. "Like me."

"Anyway, the train doesn't have to stop to get the mail, Ez," Tom said.

"It doesn't?" I asked.

He pointed. "Look."

Beside the platform was a metal post I had never noticed before. It was spindly with two short horizontal poles branching off near the top and middle. In between the poles was a gap, like where a sign might go. But there was no sign. Only a burlap bag, hung on rings.

"The mail bag," Tom said.

I slid ungracefully off the platform, landing onto the gravel beside Tom.

"No," Tom said. "No, Ez. Get back on the platform."

"Train's coming," Clara said.

I felt it, felt the rails quiver, the ground shake beneath us. There was a long deep moan in the distance.

"Get off the tracks," Tom said to me. "Now."

"I'm not saving your life again," Mr. Black said.

"Oh, let her die," Clara said. "She's so boring alive. On second thought—she'd be a terrible bore as a ghost, and then we'd be stuck with her forever. Esmé, get out of here."

Headlights splashed the tracks. It came around the corner then: glowing, huffing steam. I was surprised how real the ghost train looked. It moved slowly, steadily, but it was headed straight for the station.

"Go!" Tom said.

I scrambled back up the platform. "What's the plan then?" I said.

Tom had turned back to face the engine. "We stop the train. You get on and look for more mail."

"Maybe," Clara said, "the train doesn't stop for us."

"Then what?" I said.

"Then you hop on. What's the matter, Esmé? You've never hopped a running train before?"

The train blew its whistle, warning us to get out of the way.

"It's easy," Mr. Black said, his eyes glued to the approaching engine. "Just keep running. Jump when you're at the same speed as the train."

The train barreled at the ghosts now. It gave another chest-rattling blast. Someone applied an emergency brake, the wheels seizing up and shrieking, an ear-splitting sound that set my teeth on edge. Great orange sparks shot out from the wheels.

Tom, Clara, and Mr. Black didn't move.

Tom looked up at me, his face lit with sparks. "Ez," he said.

Clara licked her lips. She was grinning. Mr. Black looked pale and sick.

"You know whatever happens here, I'll find you," Tom said.

The train was not going to stop.

"Say you know," he shouted above its roar.

"I know!" I said.

He smiled, and I turned away from him, away from the scene on the tracks. I squeezed my eyes shut and curled against the wall of the stationhouse. I didn't hear any sound of collision, only the train's wheels, its bleating horn and bellowing engine. There was a male voice, shouting. There might have been screaming.

Then the train stopped. I knew only because the sound stopped, the squealing and blaring. The wheels halted and locked with a sigh.

I opened my eyes.

I knew it couldn't hurt them, the ghosts. I knew the train wasn't real. I knew none of them had actually died that way: hit by a train. I knew how they had died. Still, I didn't want to see it. I didn't want to know the shapes their bodies made, even if they were not in pain, even if it was temporary.

223

But when I raised my head, I couldn't see much of anything. White steam engulfed the platform. On the tracks, the train waited, panting like an animal, bleeding smoke and steam. The clouds cleared a bit, and I could see a door on the side of a train car close to me, a few cars down from the engine.

I lunged for it. There was a big iron hand rail I used to pull myself up. My feet found the two little steps that hung beneath the door, and I swung myself inside.

I had jumped into the first open car I could find. And, amazingly, it was the right one. Ash drifting in the open door stung my eyes, and the inside of the compartment was dim, but I could make out shelves in the train car, along the wall. Each shelf was the size of an apartment mailbox. My eyes watered. Through tears, I could see shapes on the floor beneath the shelves, lumpy white mounds, like piles of discarded sheets.

That was what I had thought ghosts looked like. That was what TV and movies and books and everything told me. And it was wrong. All of it was wrong. What everyone thought about ghosts—what I had believed my whole life—was wrong.

I touched one of the white heaps. It was a canvas bag, stuffed full of something. I stuck my arm in, my fingers grasping at hard little corners. One of the corners stung my skin, and I pulled my hand out. I had a paper cut on my thumb.

It was mail in the bags.

I held in my hand a fistful of envelopes, all different colors, all different sizes. I knelt on the floor of the train car, and spread them out. I didn't recognize any of the addressee names, and many of the stamps were strange to me. I chose a pale-blue envelope addressed to *Annabelle James*. I turned it over, then hesitated. This was breaking a law, opening someone's mail.

But my mother had said to remember the mail. My mother. And this letter was on a ghost train. No one else was ever going to read it, not in this lifetime.

I slipped my finger under the blue flap and tore.

The handwriting on the envelope, like on all of the envelopes, looked old-fashioned, spidery and cramped. My eyes narrowed, adjusting to the cursive and the dim lighting in the car, and then I began to read. *Dearest Annabelle*, the letter read. *It has been a week since I saw you. In that time, my heart has grown heavy, and the loss of you echoes. My cough is worse ...*

I scanned the rest. None of it made any sense to me. The letter writer missed this girl, Annabelle, was sorry they couldn't be together, and hoped his illness would end soon.

I knew it wouldn't.

I put the letter aside, and picked up another. This one was full of false-sounding optimism and reassurances to a friend about a fever spreading through a family. I read it quickly, and set it down. I had just opened a third letter and was reading about a ship, how strong the ship was, and how soon they expected to reach the end of their journey, when I felt the first wet drop.

A word blurred on the letter, the ink smudged.

Another drop marred the letter. I looked up. There was no dripping pipe on the ceiling, no leak. I looked back to the letter. It was damp with drops, the paper softening, folding over in my hands. The ink began to run, a blue pool.

The water was coming from the letter itself, I realized, beading up from the paper. And all the words were running together, the ink melting. The letter was drowning.

I heard a crackling. I looked down at the pile of mail to see a small orange flame burst from another letter, the one about the fever. The letter was on fire.

The letter in my hands was sopping and starting to fall to pieces. I threw it at the burning letter, but it did nothing to put out the flames. I stood and stamped out the burning letter with my foot.

But when I raised my shoe, there was nothing there on the floor of the train car. No ashes. No charred remains. Nothing left of the letter.

I turned to the others, dumping the mail sack out onto the floor. Dozens of letters spilled out. Hundreds. And they were all moving. The handwriting was moving. The addresses on the front were erasing themselves, *un-writing* themselves, the loops and crosses and dots scrubbed out.

The letters had been written by the dead. And the work of the dead was undoing itself as I watched, helpless.

"No," I said. "No. No. No." I snatched a letter, but it turned to blank paper in my hand. I dumped out a second mailbag, then a third one. They were blank. All the letters were blank, the words gone, the messages erased. It had happened too fast.

I had failed my mother. I couldn't put out the mail. I couldn't even read it.

There was a lurch. The floor beneath my feet slid forward, and I lost my balance, stumbling into the wall. The ghost train began to move.

"Tom!" I said. I didn't know if he had woken up, if the others had. I steadied myself and leaned out the open doorway. "Tom, the train!" My face was pushed out into thick black smoke. I fell back into the car, coughing, as the train chugged forward.

But I had seen something before the smoke cloud engulfed me: the bag of mail hanging on the post. The burlap mailbag was full.

226

I steadied myself. I hung onto the doorway, and lunged into the steam, my other arm swiping, reaching out for the bag, and meeting only empty air. My eyes burned. I tried to call for Tom, but my throat was parched with ash. I swung out my arm again, connecting with nothing.

The ghost train was starting to move, the wheels sparking on the tracks. But we were still too far from the mailbag. On my third swipe for the bag, my hand hit something, attached to the outside of the train.

It was a long piece of metal secured to the car. Maybe I could wrench it free, and use it to knock down the mailbag as we passed? I reached for the metal thing and pulled. It felt stuck, then the joints moved and it snapped into position. The piece had two ends. One stuck straight out like a lance.

The other end was a hook.

CHAPTER 21

Great-granddaughter

The pole with the mailbag loomed into view, and the hook simply snatched it as the train passed, just tore the bag from its perch. It was the perfect length. It had been designed for just this purpose: picking up the mail, without even stopping the train. I stared at the hook in wonder, then looked behind me toward the station. Mr. Black lay on the ground, struggling to get up. Tom and Clara had already risen.

"Tom," I shouted.

He seemed very far away. And the train was moving fast. Tom's lips mouthed something, but I couldn't read the words. Maybe *I'll find you*. Maybe *I'm fine*. Maybe nothing at all.

I watched until he disappeared, the train shuddering around a curve. I thought he motioned to Mr. Black and Clara. I thought they started to run after me.

I turned to the mail, the bag swinging on the end of the hook on the outside of the train. I yanked the bag up and off of the hook. The bag was surprisingly heavy, and the weight unbalanced me. I swung forward. My stomach lurched as the fingers of my free hand felt behind me for the doorframe and missed. I felt the wind, cold but threaded with ash. The tracks flashed by in strips of gravel and steel.

I was falling, falling out of the doorway, falling off the train.

I felt something on the back of my neck: a hand lifting me by the collar of my shirt, like the hook had grasped the mailbag. I was hauled back into the train. I fell onto my knees on the floor of the car, then scrambled quickly to my feet, holding the mailbag before me like a shield.

A man stood in the car. He wore heavy pants, a work shirt, and a wide-brimmed hat, all blackened with dirt. His hands trembled. He took off his hat, and his hands began to work it, fumbling around the brim, kneading it like dough. He had rescued me. He was staring at me. But that was not the strangest thing about him.

He was Chinese.

He said something to me, and I sighed. Fear left my body, replaced by regret and embarrassment. I couldn't understand him. I wouldn't be able to. He was a ghost, obviously. He wanted something from me, of course.

But I wouldn't be able to help him. And I wouldn't be able to tell him why.

"Look," I said. "I'm sorry. I can't."

His eyes widened. He spoke more adamantly. "*Zengsunnü*," he said.

That same word, a word I didn't know.

My grandmother had known the language as a child—and forgotten. My mother wanted to learn, but by the time she was old enough to ask, my grandmother didn't know many words anymore; she had lost her first language. We avoided Chinatown in New York, walking quickly past the supermarkets smelling of dried fish, the pink dragon fruit and pebbled brown lychee fruit in stalls; wanting to prevent this, just this: a stranger speaking to us in kindness, in a language we did not know.

"*Zengsunnü*," the man said again.

The train rustled around a curve. We both lost our balance, me and the ghost, swaying on the rattling floor. As the train turned, envelopes shot out from the cupboards and landed across the car—blank letters, all of them.

I tightened my grip on the mailbag. Did the letters inside still have any words? Had they unwritten themselves already? "Listen," I said to the man. "I can see you and hear you, but I can't speak to you. I can't understand you."

"*Zengsunnü*," the man repeated desperately. "*Zengsunnü*."

"I can't understand you," I said. "I'm so sorry."

He stepped forward, releasing his hat with one hand to grab my wrist.

I gasped. His grip was strong. His eyes were dark, looking straight into mine. They looked familiar. And his English was accented, but clear. "Great-granddaughter," he said. "Be brave."

A jolt. The train whipped around a corner so hard, I was thrown from my feet. I slammed against the wall, the mailbag slipping from my hand and falling open. Letters scattered over the floor. They were blank, like all the others, or quickly becoming blank, the addresses shrinking, the messages dissolving. Then a gust of smoke swept through the open train door, lifting the letters. A stream of them was sucked out the open door, into the night air.

"No!" I shouted. I struggled to my feet.

The train hissed and screamed. When I looked out the doorway, I saw sparks mixing with smoke. The letters were cast down the tracks like snow. When I looked back into the car, my great-grandfather was gone. With a gear screech, we stopped.

"Tom," I said.

I jumped down from the train and started running. I passed empty train cars. I passed the letters, running over them, not going back. Tom had stopped the train again—the ghosts had—I knew it.

But when I reached the back of the train, the smoke-blackened caboose, there was no one there. I squinted at the tracks stretching on in the distance. No Clara. No Mr. Black. No Tom. Where were they? A letter had drifted under my shoe. As I bent to pick it up, I heard whistling.

I froze, bent down to the gravel, one hand on the letter. The white of the paper seemed to waver and swim before my eyes. The whole world was white, and then it wasn't. A shadow fell over the letter.

I swerved to avoid the lantern, falling to my knees and rolling. I heard the collision of metal striking metal as the lantern hit the tracks.

"Get away from me!" I screamed.

I rolled to the edge of the rails. And then I stood and ran.

On the other side of the tracks was a forest, strange to me. I had no idea where the train had stopped. I had never come this far, even with Tom. But I plunged through the trees, branches slapping my arms and stinging my legs. All I saw in the darkness was the next black trunk looming up in front of me. All I heard was my own ragged breathing.

I became aware that I was going uphill. The forest floor rose. Soon it was so steep, I had to grab onto saplings for support. A branch sliced my leg, but I didn't look down. I launched across the top of the hill, yanking on branches and pulling myself along, then diving through the trees on the other side—more trees, only trees.

And then the trees thinned. I could see light up ahead. I slowed a bit. Maybe it was a car. Maybe I had reached the highway. But when I broke through the trees, I saw it was just a clearing, a circular meadow. The grass was high and mossy. It was only the moon I had seen, reflected off the grass, not the highway at all. The moon was the light.

And there were objects bouncing back the light, tall shapes in the grass, white and luminous. The meadow had a hush to it, as quiet as snow.

I remembered, strangely, my grandmother's garden, the only garden she had ever attempted. Most of the land around the house was barren, rocky and overgrown, but once, when I was a child and lived with her, she had cleared a patch and planted flowers. Or tried to plant flowers. All white ones.

A place to sit in at night, she had said. She had strung mirrors on the barn. *To reflect the moon*, she had said.

The Firecracker had rolled her eyes, and slammed the door to her room. I did too, listening to my sister mutter, "Who sits in a garden at night? Freak!" through the walls. But later I had crept to my window and peeked out to see our grandmother, sitting alone in the darkness in her moon garden, white shadows all around her.

Like ghosts, I had thought.

They reminded me of the moon garden—these stones in the clearing, glowing against the purple grass. But they weren't just stones. Even from the edge of the clearing, I could tell that they had names. They were tombstones: plain graves, with a name and date only. Some had no names, only *RIP*. Some of the letters had worn away. I felt pulled to the stones, pulled by the names. When I read the first one, I saw why.

WONG.

I read my own last name.

"Rail man's graveyard." The Stationmaster stepped into the clearing, lantern swinging at his side. I backed up until the tombstone was between us, though it barely came up to my waist.

"Dangerous work," the Stationmaster said, "what we did. Did you know that, little girl? It was hard, working for the railroad. A man could get killed. A man could get maimed. A man could lose his legs. A man could lose his arms, and bleed to death, right there on the track before help came." He nodded at the stone. "That's what happened to your great-grandpappy."

I felt the blood in my body freeze. I felt the old burns on my hand turn to ice. "What do you mean?"

"He didn't make it," the Stationmaster said. "Because he couldn't listen. Couldn't hear the order to *Get up, get out of the way. Train's coming!*" He waved his hat, grinning. "Because he didn't know English, you see. He didn't understand. Learn English, little girl. That's your first lesson in manners."

I stared at him steadily. "I'm American."

"Lesson two: don't speak until spoken to." He raked the lantern across my great-grandfather's tombstone, dragging the rusted metal over the stone with a slow, teeth-jarring scratch.

I winced. I became aware of a presence beside me, someone not quite touching my shoulders: ribbons, white-blond hair. Clara. A presence, a feeling, on the other side of me too. Mr. Black.

"Where's Tom?" I whispered.

Clara shook her head.

"The Stationmaster doesn't want you," I said to her. "You don't have to be here. He wants me."

"I want you to behave," the Stationmaster said. "I want you to be better. I will make you be better."

"Run!" Clara said.

"No," I resisted. "You all can't keep saving me."

There was a tearing sound, and the unmistakable smell of sulfur; the Stationmaster had lit a match on his shoe. He held the flame up, flickering, let it burn down to his fingers. He flicked the blackened match away, then struck another.

Clara flinched.

"Right," Mr. Black said to her. "You stay out of this then."

The Stationmaster struck a third match. One of them would ignite the grass, I knew. One of them would light the fire to kill Clara, kill her again.

I said the only question to him I could think of, the one I had asked a dozen times now. "What do you want?"

The Stationmaster laughed.

"How many kids have you killed?"

He lit a fourth match, and stared at me, the red glow bloodying his face. "Enough to like it."

Mr. Black leapt toward the Stationmaster, pushing me out of the way. I was shoved against the tombstone of my ancestor, my breath knocked from my lungs. Clara cried out, and I turned to see the last match setting the grass on fire.

The fire spread quickly, dry grass rustling as it blazed. I crawled on my hands and knees to Clara, slumped with her back against a tombstone. Across the clearing, Mr. Black fought with the Stationmaster.

"He does this to me," Clara said. "He provokes me. He made me set the fire in the house. He wanted me to."

"I know, I know," I said. I put my arm around her shoulder. She was shaking, so small. How had I never noticed how small she was? She was younger than me, I reminded myself. She was—and always would be—a child.

I crouched, keeping Clara close to me, and the two of us crept behind the tombstones. I could hear shouting and clanging as the lantern struck stone. The fire burned red and fast around the Stationmaster and Mr. Black. Clara and I stumbled out of the graveyard, into the cover of the trees. Clara was as limp and docile as a doll, but once we made it into the woods, she shook off my arm and broke away from me.

"What's wrong?" I asked.

"My death," she said. "I want it."

"You can't go back there."

"You don't understand."

"Clara!" I said.

But she was already gone, thrashing through the trees, back to the clearing. Smoke threaded through the forest. My eyes stung, my lungs constricting. Then I heard a whistle.

Not the Stationmaster. The train.

Remember the mail, I heard my mother say. Why wouldn't she tell me something that would protect me that would save me?

I heard the whistle again. That meant it was close. The train whistled like that—even the ghost train—as a warning when it pulled into a station.

Or a tunnel.

I followed the sound. I began to run, not feeling the branches as they whipped my limbs and face, not smelling the smoke. My whole world filled with the sound of the whistle, until with a lunge, I broke through the trees.

The tunnel stood ahead, to my left, the tunnel where Tom had taken me; I recognized the high, vandalized walls. I followed them, running alongside the tracks. I could hear the train, but couldn't see it. I began to worry that I was too late, that I had missed it.

Something was in the tunnel, though.

Someone.

I ran into the mouth. It was black outside, night, but it was blacker within the closed walls of the tunnel. As my eyes adjusted, I saw the figure I had seen come into focus: long arms, legs balanced, neck extended.

My mother.

My mother danced in the train tunnel again.

My eyes filled with tears.

In the dreams—or visions or hauntings—she had never looked at me. Not once. She closed her eyes, concentrating, as she did in all the pictures I had seen of her dancing. She seemed to see no one, to be aware of nothing but the dance. Like my grandmother, listening for the dead. I didn't expect anything different from this dream, this vision, this haunt. But still I walked toward her onto the tracks.

She opened her eyes. She stopped dancing, relaxing her position, shaking out her arms and legs. She was my height exactly, I realized. She was just like me. Or I was like her. She reached her arm above her head. She stretched. She looked at me.

"I'm so proud of you, Esmé," she said.

The light came from behind her, the light I had always seen. In my visions, I mistook it for a spotlight, but I knew now what it was.

"The train. It's coming!" I rushed forward to push her out of the way, to save her—and tripped, falling into open air. My mother was gone.

I had fallen on my knees between the tracks, and raised my head to face the train's headlight. But the light didn't grow bigger, as the train approached. And the light was swinging, bouncing off the tunnel walls. It wasn't a train headlight at all, I realized.

It was the light in a lantern.

I didn't have the energy to stand. Maybe my mother had come to help me die. Maybe she was proud of me for making it this far, at least. I watched the dancing light, waiting for the Stationmaster to appear around the curve. I wasn't going to fight him, not again. I couldn't. I didn't have the strength.

I heard a whistle.

But the sound came from behind me. I forced myself to look, though turning caused some muscle I didn't know I had to ache. There was the headlight, there was the steam, there was the roaring, monstrous train.

It was my mail train.

"I caught you," the Stationmaster's voice reverberated off the walls. "I always do."

I wondered what had happened to Tom, to Mr. Black. I wondered if Clara had run into the flames again, if Tom had been beaten until his body lay still.

I spoke into the lantern's light. "Who hurt you?" I asked. "What was done to you?"

The Stationmaster came around the curve. I could see him by the light of his own lantern. He was just a man. An old man. Dead.

"Nothing," he said.

"You were an orphan." I managed to stand. "You were lawless. You were friendless. You were from bad blood." I heard the train behind me. The wind pushed my hair into my face. I stepped from the track, inched to the side. Every step ached. "You're the one," I said. "It's you that needs help."

He was coming closer, striding down the very center of the train tracks.

"*You* need manners," I said.

"Little girl."

"*You* need discipline."

"I'm warning you."

"*You* need supervision."

The tunnel was awash in blinding light. The train was a roar, and it was here, here, everywhere at once, filling the tunnel. The tracks shook. We were going to be struck by it, killed by it, both of us. We were going to be mowed down.

I was going to die.

And I wanted to live. I wanted to be seen again, seen by my grandmother and sister, by my friends. I wanted to make new friends. I wanted to figure out my gift, who I was, who my ancestors had been, the women of my family. I wanted to live. I wanted to live. I remembered the safety bays Tom had shown to me, the recesses in the wall for ducking down when a train approached.

But there wasn't time to find one. I squeezed against the wall, making myself as flat as I could. The space between the wall and the track was so narrow, my toes touched the rail. So I turned my feet to the side, making them parallel to the track. I flung my arms out, embracing the wall behind my back. I was in second position, I realized, my body stretched against the bricks in a stance I had seen my mother and sister do so many times, but had never bothered to try myself; I had never wanted to. All the ballet I had been forced to sit through, all the dancing I had never done—would it save me now?

The train was rattling by me, shaking and roaring. My teeth trembled. My skull quaked. Wind threw grit and gravel in my hair. I felt the train in my bones.

Even as the engine tore through beside us, the Stationmaster reached for me. He would take me down with him, drag me back onto the tracks. He would kill me. He didn't fear death; he was already dead.

His hand clamped my wrist. With his other, he raised his lantern.

"You need supervision!" I screamed above the train.

And then I ducked.

There was a slicing sound, like the lantern swinging through air. But it was the sound of a hook, the mail hook on the side of the train, cutting off cleanly the Stationmaster's head.

CHAPTER 22

Free

Tom found me in the tunnel. As we walked out together, the ghost train disappeared. It just vanished from the tracks.

"The Stationmaster went away like that," I said. "I didn't look, but I felt it. He was there, then he wasn't. Just wasn't. It made a gusting sound."

Tom nodded as if he understood.

"I don't think he'll come back, this time," I said. "It feels different. I don't ... sense him anymore. I think this was what he needed—what he wanted—all along, to have someone hold him accountable, to call him out, to yell at him, to punish *him*. He wanted to be caught."

Tom helped me over the tracks. "How did you think to do that?"

"Remember Clara and the hot chocolate? Grandma said it's the thought that counts."

He smiled. I could see his grin flashing in the darkness, and then I noticed the dark wasn't as dark as I remembered. Gray light filtered between the trees, and the sky above them was navy-colored. It was almost dawn.

We left the tunnel, walking beside the track, the tall walls rising up on either side of us, twenty feet or taller, majestic, though they were crumbling and scarred. I became aware of a rustling on top of the walls. I looked up to see a shadow standing there at the edge of the forest. It was a boy.

"Who is that?" I asked.

Another rustling. Another figure stood on the opposite side.

More figures appeared to stand on the top of the tunnel walls. They had come from the woods, and stood silently at the tree line, shoulder to shoulder. They flanked both sides. They stood looking straight ahead, an honor guard for us, marking the way.

They were ghosts.

"Children," I said.

"Kids who wanted what you did, to catch the Stationmaster, to stop him."

As we passed them, the ghosts faded, one by one, as suddenly as they had appeared.

"They got what they wanted," I whispered. "They're free."

There was another surprise for us: Clara stood at the top of the hill in front of my grandmother's house, dawn breaking over her face.

"Are you all right?" I asked. "Did you die again?"

She shrugged. "Last time, I think. Once more, for the memories, you know."

Behind her, people and ghosts were coming out of the house, my grandmother and Martha, the Firecracker and Mr. Black. They seemed very small and far away.

I stood where I was, and stared at Clara. The sun was coming over the hills, and I could see it reflected golden in her eyes, the first glimmer of light I had seen there, I realized. "You seem different," I said.

241

"It's over. He's gone. The man who killed me and my brother is gone."

"But that's not what you wanted."

"That is." She pointed, and I looked behind me, at Tom grinning as wide as I had ever seen him. He held out his hand and I took it.

Clara sighed. "I suspect you'll go to hell, Esmé, so I imagine I won't see you." She looked down through her lashes. "But until then, have some fun for me, will you? Promise me you'll try it, that fun thing, while you're still alive?"

"I'll try," I said.

She flicked her hair and half turned, as if she was going to greet the group coming down from the house. She raised her knee to skip. Then she vanished, into the hill, into the grass. She just turned and faded, like a light switched off.

"Clara!" I said. I felt Tom's fingers lacing tight in mine.

"It's all right," he said. "I think it's all right."

"What's happening now?"

"Now," he said, "I think your grandmother's business falls away sharply."

"Excuse me?" my grandmother said. "Was that the drunk one?"

"Ma'am, I beg your pardon," Mr. Black said. "I am the drunk one. At least, I was drunk yesterday." He frowned. "And the day before. And ... one hundred and something years prior. But today," he raised his index finger, "today I have not touched a drop."

Martha slid to his side, slipping her arm through his.

"Kiss her," Tom said.

"Oh yes," Mr. Black said. He cleared his throat. He lifted his hand to Martha's face, to touch her cheek and draw her close.

"Oh, is this what it's like then?" she said.

"Yes," Mr. Black said. He bent his face to hers.

Martha smiled until her eyes shone, then closed her eyes for the kiss, then—

"No!" I said. "Wait!"

They were gone. They were gone together. They were sunlight. They were air.

I sank onto my knees on the hill.

"What's happening?" the Firecracker said.

"We need to go," my grandmother said, touching my sister's shoulder, and turning her away. "Make breakfast, make ourselves useful. Esmé's going to need us." They trudged off to the house, my grandmother looking back over her shoulder once—almost at me, I thought. But it couldn't be.

"I'm still invisible," I said.

Tom sat down on the grass beside me. "I don't think it's permanent. You have a gift. It's a little hard at first. But you're getting practice."

"I'll be out of practice soon," I said. Now Clara was gone, Mr. Black, Martha ...

"Don't forget the Builder," Tom said. "He's going to need a lot of convincing that that house of his is done. That could take years."

I groaned. "That's never gonna work."

"You have a big gift, Ez," Tom said. "But you'll grow into it."

"This is a very awkward growing stage. Much worse than getting taller. Which I'll probably also never do."

"You will get taller," Tom said. "And grow old. And fall in love."

"I already did that," I said. "I think I already did."

"Me too."

My voice was a whisper. "What's going to happen now?"

"I don't know," Tom said.

"Will I be able to see you? Or hear you? Or sense you?"

"I don't know."

"Will we find each other again?"

"Yes," he said. "Of that, I'm certain." He put my chin in his hand, and tilted my head like Mr. Black and Martha. My eyes flickered up until they were looking into his. More color had come into his face. More light had reached his eyes. He looked more alive now than ever, now that he was drifting from me, now that he was almost ready to go.

I felt the tips of my own fingers tingling, like blood was returning to them after they had been asleep. I felt a flush in my chest.

"Tom Griffin," I said. "I love you."

"I don't think that goes away," he said. "I don't think any of that feeling goes away, ever. No matter what happens or doesn't happen or can never happen. I love you. That lives with you."

He kissed me, one of the those kisses that goes on forever, one of those kisses I had never had before—and only a few times since—the kind that causes the sun to come fully over the hill, the clouds to turn colors, the birds begin to sing. Dawn rose in the sky, and warmed it. When morning light hit my skin, I could feel it—and when I reached to touch Tom, I couldn't.

He was there. I knew he was there, somehow, somewhere, some part of him. I could feel him still: in the grass of the hill, in the summer light and the singing birds, in the tear-shaped leaves, in the birches. But I couldn't see him. I couldn't hear him. Was this my gift? Just knowing I wasn't alone—no one was—knowing the dead were still with us, that they were always with us?

It wasn't a *just*. It was everything.

I sat for a long time on the hill, being comforted with Tom's presence, Tom's memory, Tom's love. And then I went inside, where my grandmother had spotted me through the window.

Acknowledgements

Thank you to my family: Nancy and Herman Stine, Andrew Stine and Katie Berki, and Ashley Stine and Andy Bachman. Thank you to my wonderful agent Carol Mann, to my editors Rachel Winterbottom and Natasha Bardon, and to everyone at Harper*Voyager*. I am grateful to all of my friends, and thank the following people especially for their assistance, inspiration, and encouragement with this project: Geri Lipschultz, Ellee Prince, Brad Daugherty, Matt Glass, Angel Lemke, Marlene Tromp, Jordan Davis, and Jeff VanderMeer (my first and only fiction teacher). Thank you to my students over the years, especially to the writers at the Denison University Jonathan R. Reynolds Young Writers Workshop. To my fellow faculty and teaching assistants there: you have become like family, and I am lucky to have you in my life. Thank you to my book brothers and sisters at Harper*Voyager*. Thank you most of all to Henry and James.

I wrote *Supervision* in the Rose Main Reading Room at the New York Public Library on 42nd Street in Manhattan. And to the library security guards who, over the course of a year, became my friends, and gave me support, company, and tough love: this book is for you too. You told me to go after my dream. Because of a public library, this book was written—and I encourage everyone, after finishing it, to find their own dreams in a library.